A Peep into the 20th Century

Also by Christopher Davis

ISHMAEL

THE SHAMIR OF DACHAU

BELMARCH

A KIND OF DARKNESS

FIRST FAMILY

LOST SUMMER

A
PEEP
INTO THE
20th CENTURY

Christopher Davis

HARPER & ROW, PUBLISHERS

New York • Evanston • San Francisco • London

To my mother and father

I owe thanks to Mr. and Mrs. Lithgow Osborne, Mr. and Mrs. Frederik Osborne, and Mr. W. O. Dapping of Auburn, New York, for their help; also to Daniel McMann, Warden of Auburn Prison, and other prison staff. John P. Meehan, Stephen E. Davis, Eric Sellin, David I. Segal, and others offered counsel, for which I thank them. Part of this novel was written under a grant from the National Endowment for the Arts, and I am grateful to the Endowment.

one

Weber's Silence

1

Now he did not sleep at all; at least it seemed to him that he did not.

Keeper Kernahan yawned—or McDade: a gasping yawn of deep tiredness, the breath taken in in sections like rope being hauled. The keeper, whichever it was—well, he knew Kernahan was night watch—rose and stretched, his magazine slipping to the floor, making a big shadow on the distempered wall, waving around the glasses he had pulled off so that they jumped like a grasshopper at the end of the shadow's paw. Anyhow the image of the insect presented itself if Weber did not make the comparison. He saw they were plain spectacles all right. He saw the lenses turn over flat, then go round and shine out. Yawning and stretching; the coming of dawn as the fields and cities turned into the sun. His window high up in the wall showed dark and light separate, the night drop like a tide leaving one or two rayed stars visible: this was passed over by Weber, looked over solemnly with only an old image left in his mind of flood water dropping low on a meadow.

It was over: it was nothing.

Silence was inside Weber as well as out. His movements were effortlessly silent; not his bedclothes, not the clothing he wore so much as whispered.

On the table, which was bolted to the floor, were the pictorial Bible Snow had given him, and the Common Prayer, the pigs-in-clover puzzle, the cards he had autographed; he did not touch them now and only looked them over in that smooth way, putting them under his silence, which was like dust falling. Mostly he did not even trouble to turn his head. He had not when they used the machine to kill a veal as a test on the day of his reprieve, sixteen hours before the hour he had expected to die. But he had not been silent then. That began with the news that he need not die so soon.

2

Mrs. Buxton resumed her visits at once after the reprieve. It was always just about eleven in the morning when she appeared, and sun reached the window opposite Weber's cage at that hour in those spring weeks, so that the warden's wife appeared to bring it with her. It struck through the window down into Weber's cage where it touched the table's still objects and a corner of the bed beyond. During her stay it moved up the bed and off it, gleamed on the rim and handle of the water cup on its shelf, moved out of the cage, and onto the grated door of the neighboring cage; it grew hot, focused in the rubble of the window's corner, then left.

Chaplain Snow took Weber's bunk. The convict was on the stool, bony hands clasped around his knees; while his eyes ranged abstractedly, he rocked back and forth. Silence lay everywhere thick and dusty. When no one spoke in these lower deep-walled cells silence was heavy anyhow; but now Weber sat in the center of that quiet putting his own will to silence on everything like a seal. There was a slate on the table upon which he had put his name and "Clarkville, April 30, 1890"—the date on the death warrant. "First man in history to die under law by electricity," Weber had added with the keeper's help.

He'd made his profession of faith and been baptized a month before. At the convict's own request Snow administered the Sacrament of the Lord's Supper on April 29th in the forenoon, he and Reverend Baird from town bringing bread and a covered pewter cup full of sweet wine. Now he would not speak to the chaplain.

4

A handful of people, mostly men and boys, had stood at the prison gates, but when the reporters came out and went across the street to the depot where the new telegraph office was situated the handful grew quickly into a crowd, which followed the correspondents down Empire Street under the new-budding elms and over the bridge—men and youngsters running down the slope toward the Clark House: "Say, has he been touched off? Is he gone?"

Most had been convinced that Rupert Weber was dead and discounted the rumor of the reprieve. "How did he die? Who did it?" Those had been the main points in their minds. Did he die bravely? Which of the electricians put his hand to the switch? They had wanted to know that man's name.

5

"Oh, Rupert."

His eyes passed over her, then returned alertly but with a preoccupied expression. It was as if he had forgotten something he meant to say but would think of in just a moment. From the farm garden outside the west wall of the prison came an easy country sound of a farmer speaking to his team: a creak and jingle of harness and the pleasant warm cries of the man.

Mrs. Buxton missed a day and came in on the Saturday.

"Chaplain Snow is worried by your silence," she said.

His silence had already become famous in the prison.

McDade, the day watch, looked on from the entrance to his cubicle. Weber sat with arms folded across his chest, one leg cocked across the other, foot bobbing. He had a parrot's face, yellowish with a beaky nose between blue eyes, sunken cheeks; yet he was handsome in a certain way.

"I wish you would talk to him. He says you no longer look in your Bible."

6

" 'In a word, our Heavenly life should commence when we are baptised, day by day ought we to grow in grace, and when we have grown sufficiently, God takes us to the Upper Room above,' " Mrs. Buxton read aloud. " 'It is this mistake of separating Heaven and earth which makes people careless of their lives. If you want to dwell with God through all eternity, you must humbly dwell with God all the days of your earthly life. Look again through the open door, and learn that in Heaven God is the central figure. So, if we are living here as Christ's people, God will be the central figure in *our* life, the Alpha and Omega, the beginning and the end of all our work, our wish, our plan. My brothers, if you feel that with you *self* is the chief object in your existence, be sure that you are not living the Heavenly life. You have put yourself in the place of God.' "

7

McDade stopped by the cage, portly and white-thatched, his steel-rimmed spectacles folded into his workingman's hand. The day watch thought of himself as a plain workingman. Kernahan had been on for only three months, but McDade had stayed the year through with all the appeals and newspaper noise, the hearings and resentencings—the State's whole circus. He had seen men hanged, and it was bad enough; but he had no faith in this thing, this rig of wires. The latest calf died promptly, yet McDade had watched one totter and walk after 700 volts and another breathe for ten minutes after 1,000. If it went like a charm, was "humane," as they contended, as the papers and the Wizard said it was sure to be, it was wrong, McDade knew. You did not wire a man into a rig like a fly in a web, and stick electrodes on patches where the skin had been shaved, pull down a switch, and roast him like a pig, and call that humanity. No.

He looked into the cage.

"Kernahan didn't take your bucket when he went off, did he?"

McDade would do it. Carrying Weber's bucket gave him pleasure, though he would be ashamed to admit it.

Then he forgot too and walked up and down tapping his loaded stick into the palm of his beefy hand until the odor from the bucket reminded him. It was all like Cody's redskin circus, he thought, these goings-on—the State's high jinks, the companies' fancy shuffles and deals.

He held inward discourse, putting people—Warden Buxton, Fox, Mr. Westinghouse for the delays, Mr. Edison, the lawyers and judges—all in their places, putting people where they belonged.

The odor reminded him of the job. Weber did not move his bowels more than once a week; now here it was, and Kernahan had walked off. Well, it was all right.

Mrs. Buxton would appear and read out of her book of sermons like a parson; then Chaplain Snow, unhappy, hurt by the man's unwillingness to speak after all the work he'd done—mooning and sighing: though that wasn't fair, he supposed. But Mrs. Buxton could take the train down to New York, as she had done this time, go to a hotel, be asleep elsewhere at dawn while Weber was rigged into his net of wires. And McDade could not do that.

8

" 'Again, as we look through the open door,' " Mrs. Buxton read from *The Life of Duty*, " 'we see the intense *beauty* of the Heavenly life. We see gates of pearl, and a throne on which sits one like a jasper and a sardine stone, and the rainbow round about the throne is in sight like unto an emerald. . . .' "

9

The barber was a lifer named Stern.

"Well, so you have one more reprieve, Weber."

Night watchman Kernahan, who did not go off until midmorning, sat observing. He wore a ring on the small finger of each hand, and they winked in the new light.

"We're behind you," the barber said easily. "I have had a number of kites for you and have brought some along."

Weber said nothing.

"The loonies over the wall in the annex, you know, were a great deal exercised on Tuesday when they thought you were to be taken off. There was near a riot over there, and they had to put on more guards. No one was supposed to know, but they knew it and knew what time it was to be too. Right, Mr. Kernahan? They just got them calmed down when news of your writ come through, and this started the other half of them yelling. It's lucky you can't hear them here. In a way it's comical.

"And I was led to understand I wouldn't be giving this man his shaves no more, yet you see me here. How do you account for it, Mr. Kernahan?"—not expecting a reply. He worked for a time without speaking. Occasionally he would glance up in his deep-lidded lifer's way at the keeper. "We're all saying Weber's among the living yet!" he went on finally. "Don't count him out." Working rapidly, voice rising or dropping to a whisper, he created a world that included guard and prisoner separately, so that he could prevent one from knowing what he said to the other. "The opinion upstairs is that it will succeed this time; they've kept you hanging fire too long, and it's few who get their case to the U.S. Court. The cruel and unusual aspect has done it, Weber, because that's against both the constitution of the State and of the country. We're persuaded it's going to work and that you'll be discharged, so keep your chin up.

"Kernahan," said Stern in what seemed just the same voice, "I have got one or two kites of congratulation here for the prisoner, and I hope you won't object if I leave them."

10

McDade came on, and Kernahan went up into the yard with Weber's bucket, and thrust his way in among the line of prisoners who were carrying their slop pails to the King's Palace. When he emptied Weber's bucket he saw that there was nothing in it but the notes the barber had brought still screwed up small. Then he saw briefly looking up at him from the stream that carried the waste away John the Baptist in his camel's-skin coat holding an infant Jesus.

11

The mood of the prison was lightened by news of Weber's re-prieve.

At night before lights-out a convict played a cornet. Its music came into the yard and down into Weber's cage. Other prisoners with musical instruments gave the cornet a chance first because it was good, then they came in: violins, harmonicas, jew's-harps. Someone sang:

> You do refuse to give your heart?
> Then give back mine to me!

After lights-out the clicking and tapping of prisoners' messages ran down the walls into Weber's basement cage. There were the bells from the Town Hall clock to be heard every quarter hour, and long sad whistles and crossing bells from the Central's main branch. But silence stood both outside and in Weber, heavy and deaf, as if he lay under deep water. Kernahan's magazine would slip from his knee and the night watch rise and stretch, a shadow of the glasses he and McDade shared by keeping them in a drawer in their cubicle crawling across the wall. Now and then at two or three in the morning Weber would pace without sound. Except for brief fragments of dreams, shocks that made him sit straight up staring, he did not sleep. He did not need sleep any more than he needed to use his bucket, that is rarely and briefly. He did not need anything much. He had had little sexual desire in the last ten of the seventeen months since his arrest, not since Snow first began to lead him toward baptism. In those first months he had used desire secretly each night with a hand to get himself to sleep, and he had slept then. But after Snow began to interest him—since then—there had been almost nothing. And now there was nothing.

"He is naturally upset by the events to date. The cycle of hope and disappointment has worn him down so that the inward man is resting up so to speak, asleep in fact. I am certain he will come out of it."

"His silence . . ."

"He was always laconic," Prison Physician Clark said.

"He doesn't utter a word."

"Well, he will, you know. Children play this same game and find they have to speak at last."

"I hope you are right," Snow said.

"We'll see if I am. I think your opinion is that this is a symptom of disease in the soul. I don't say it's not, but I draw the distinction under the circumstances. Science concerns itself with the possibility of madness. If on examination of this symptom and others he is judged mad by a qualified committee, and if the disease appears to be of a lasting or worsening nature, as far as these things can be told, then the man's sentence may be commuted, and we put him in the asylum. This is a concern of law and science. Well, but what about his soul?" Clark asked when the other frowned. "Does your profession admit madness there?"

"No. Weber is not crazy," said Snow.

Science was Snow's temptation. What Clark said had struck him. "It is not a question of madness in his case but of darkness, and I mean to say that that is *everything* in the end—what I'd call a man's moral darkness. After the first resentencing he seemed dazed, but this is not the same; he was not morose then. I know he is a man of small mental caliber, and I wish it were otherwise, since it is my job to reach him again. I was certain we had cast light there until now."

"Don't you think that in a modern society we might not commute the capital sentence of a man unprepared to meet his maker?" Then Clark said in a repentant tone, "He will do very well, Hannibal, believe me. Only stay as constant and patient as you've been."

He offered to say a word to Weber.

"He may respond to you."

Chaplain Snow was what—thirty? Certainly no more than that, possibly less. He had a young pretty wife and three pretty little girls. Clark had been on several earlier occasions to Sunday dinner at Snow's house: a pleasant, many-gabled old farm structure of weatherboard and stone that the town had surrounded. Hedges of yew and lilac grew around the front yard, roses and arbor vitae along the old stone fence in back—as pleasant as could be. Mrs. Snow wore her dark blond hair in plaits pinned around her head and blushed when she was addressed, which tickled Clark. They played tennis and croquet on the front lawn in view of the town and lake because Snow was a liberal in his profession. Today Mrs. Snow had on pale linen and looked a picture, her tiny foot pressed on the bright striped ball as she prepared to hit it, a warm afternoon putting dew on her upper lip, a pretty screw of hair falling over her forehead. The children sat on cane chairs drinking lemonade, one in dark blue, one in pink, the littlest in yellow. Snow, who had evening service ahead of him, wore dark clothes and was solemn playing the game, but Clark spun his mallet in his big country hands like a baton.

13

"Reverend Snow feels this. He is worried about you, Weber. As far as I am concerned you may be silent for a month or a year or for whatever remains of your life, but Reverend Snow wants to talk to you about your spiritual state. Now here he is waiting. Shan't you be friends again, Rupert?

"You must know that this reprieve puts off the end for a very short time and that soon all will be as it was ten days ago. Your lawyers and whoever is paying them (we are sure that you are not) for reasons of their own have seen fit to secure you a further period of uncertainty, of anxiety. You spoke to a lawyer about this and put your name on a petition. Why not? No one is going to blame you for trying. It might be held odd if you didn't.

". . . as far as my own calling and interest are involved you are in the pink."

At Weber's table leafing through the pictorial Bible, Snow said, "As far as mine are involved too . . ."

"But you're troubled by his refusal to speak, Hannibal, whereas I am not." He raised his voice: "Your very good friend is troubled, Weber. Won't you vouchsafe him something to go on with—a little fuel for the conversational engine? In my own opinion you had prepared so well with Mr. Snow's help that the sudden news threw you into some sort of neutral state. When you are good and ready, provided we have behaved ourselves in the meantime, you shall speak—right, Weber? We must earn confidence according to your unspoken standard. There's your old comrade, Sergeant McDade. No word for him either? . . . Here, look at me."

He turned the prisoner's narrow face into the light, pushed up each eyelid in turn with his big thumb, and searched the pale blue irises. For a second time he took out his watch and pinched Weber's wrist. McDade looked on from outside the cage. Warden Buxton came down the short iron staircase, through the room where the chair stood and the guards' cubicle, and paused beside McDade.

Weber's pulse beat sixty-six times in one minute.

"You are a calm chap," said Clark. "What I think is that you are becalmed, in fact. The wind has dropped right out of your sails with this reprieve, and you discover yourself in unknown, rather: unexpected waters. He is becalmed."

They looked at him in his deep silence.

Warden Buxton carried an envelope. "This is usurping your office, Mr. Snow, but I feel sure that you will not mind in this case, and it may serve as Clark's wind."

He offered the envelope through the open door of the cage, and Weber glanced at it and then briefly up at Buxton's chalky features. He did not take it, and his eyes slid abstractedly away as if he were trying to pick up some thread of thought.

"It's from your brother in Philadelphia. He has written to you —a perfectly grand letter!"

They all—McDade, Clark, Snow, Buxton—stood off and watched him.

14

Mrs. Buxton came with the sunshine. *The Life of Duty* was in her workbag, but now she left it there.

"I know that you've had news from home."

She had been beside the lake earlier, as she had gone each day for a week, to see if the apple trees had bloomed.

"I heard an oriole warble today. He's the first of the year, I think, to come back.

"It's splendid that your brother has written you at last!"

Mrs. Buxton sighed, her head lowered so that she looked up at the prisoner. She was tired by her pity, by her observation of the cruelty of men. She could not see that her pity accomplished much, and it hurt her to think that she was made to feel it so bitterly, with such power to tire and even injure her, without its being of the least use.

The bird had sung with all its small strength. The apple blossoms, barely begun, were a pale green web caged in the old branches. She had felt young for a moment and famished as once she might have been for spring weeks on end. But all the while the thought of the man Weber lay coiled. She looked down from the little pier like a dreaming girl, saw the green spring dusting on the inlet that swept under her feet and the bright deltas where snags caught the water; like a girl she felt spring sunshine on her shoulders through the cotton of her dress: alive, she sang with the oriole; but all the while the man lay coiled inside her like something to come: a prognostication: a birth to come in term, or a cancer.

15

May 2, 1890

DEAR BRO:

It must suprise you to have some word of me after these many months. It is promted by news of your reprieve. We offer wishes for good word from our high court and are certain that Justice will be finally tempered by mercy. We are well. I do not speak of your wife except to say she holds no Grudge, and forgives all, which I atest. I speak no more of that or your crime. A crime affects many and provokes mischief everywhere, God knows. You would not think, would you, that a crime done in Buffalo as yours affects those down in Phila? the family of the criminal is in disgrace too and bears up as well as it may. I don't say it to cause you further uneasiness, knowing well the suffering you endure thus far, but to atest that I am not now ashamed before God or my neibors of Rupert Weber, and I aknowledge you before all. The paper says you are baptised with God's grace. It may suprise you to know that some years ago in secret I too was baptised. I blame our fathers neglect of this rite for much that came afterwards of ill to our family. You can not neglect Gods demands without direst consequences, *esp to children*. Put all your trust in Gods compassion. Tell Him the truth about *everything* when you pray. Tell the whole truth, and trust in Gods Minister who comes in the bowels of compassion to prevent you falling into despair. I often remember our *hard* childhood. I remember how our father came back from the War a different man. I blame him for much of our ills, but maybe I am in the wrong here. You are famous in Phila and the argument about the alternating and direct current is the rage. I praise Fox and the Committee for their law to make this delivery of a soul to God instant and painless. If it comes to it have no fear. I have none for you, Rupert, and remain now as always.

Your Affect Bro
A. H. WEBER

16

Keeper Kernahan had his supper at eleven in the morning, slept until five or six in the afternoon, ate breakfast, and took a walk or went down to the lake to fish for perch and bass. Sometimes he watched boys play baseball in the lakeside park and now and then played himself on the police and prison guard nine against a hose company or one of the union teams. He was what his few companions called a sport. He owned a new Columbia bicycle and would ride it through the streets of Clarkville, straight-backed and slim, his near-bald freckled head held alertly high, cycling up newly paved North Line or Empire, across the new-laid electric trolley car tracks on Exchange, down to the lakeside, back on South Line past the *Advertiser* office where, like McDade, he had had his portrait cut, and home to the boardinghouse on Schuyler Street, where he lived alone, to take his nap at eight in the evening before going onto the death watch.

He kept his thoughts mostly to himself but would talk to the correspondents any time they wanted. When a newspaperman asked if assisting at executions troubled him, he stared hard at him, frowning. "You ain't serious, are you? That's my job. It troubles me as much as eating a meal does, or a day's work would another man, that's all. Are you serious?" He expected at least a meal in payment for the interview and for answering this question that every newsman asked him, often more than once as if in the hope that his reply might alter. But he liked the press well enough and usually had something for them. On the day after Weber got his letter he said to Chaney, the *New York Times* man who had come into town for a day and was treating Kernahan to his late morning supper, "It was the finest representation in the Bible which Reverend Snow give him as a gift—a lovely colored picture of John the Baptist with baby Jesus and the dove flying down. I won't tell you what he done with it, and you couldn't print it in your paper anyhow, but I'll just say it wound up in his slops pail. He got kites from his fellow cons saying they was pleased at his reprieve, and that's where they wound up too—in the pail; and a letter from his brother, the only one he ever got from him—that was in the bucket this morning.

"No, he ain't pretending to be a kink. I know him. I know him better than McDade does, though I've been less than half the time McDade has in his pleasant company. He is as sane as you or I. He is a hard uncaring man—a murderer and drunkard, you know—taking a hatchet to a girl he run away with to Buffalo; he is stupid but not crazy. He is working on something in his mind, and it will come out sooner or later."

And to the same man: "I believe it is just getting through to him that he will die before his time, and what that means."

two

Is Absalom Safe?

1

Snow's method had been to choose a text from the Bible or Common Prayer and multiply illustrations until he was sure the man had taken it all in. He would not offer more than one point at a time, and he worried each point like a terrier. It was gospel applied, and it had appeared to work. Snow had even taught him to read a little and to write his name. If his moral perceptions were of a low order yet the chaplain was certain Weber had attained something like an intelligent knowledge of the gospel way of salvation: an intelligent trust in Christ.

Snow held his discussion group as usual after chapel.

"I think that this delay may do more harm than good," he said to these men confidingly. He had addressed them concerning Weber before this when he was pleased with his work with him or troubled, and he had kept them abreast of things during the electrical execution hearings of the previous summer. Soberly they had discussed all the proposed techniques for capital execution and finally championed the electrical method. They had been avid to talk of electricity in any form, Snow, who was fascinated by the science and even performed experiments at home, foremost among them. He bought books on the subject and showed them to the men, and brought in Leyden jars and glass tubes and other paraphernalia so that they could duplicate some of the experiments. They talked about amperes, and volts, and the different kinds of current, the core of the present controversy over Weber.

"With All My Heart" was worked in gold and scarlet letters a foot high on one side of the chapel platform, "The Lord Is My Shepherd" on the other; above: "Glory To God In The Highest." There were blue and pink and yellow squares of glass among the panes in the windows, and the men sat in the light from these and ran their hands through the colored shafts as if they could feel them.

"It don't have anything to do with constitutionality, that's all my eye," one of the convicts offered, sensing as he always did the chaplain's view. "That was worked over in the hearings and decided on. Westinghouse is frightened of the poor sales if his alternating machine is used."

"And don't that suit Edison? It's why he set it up here."

Snow did not contradict either man.

"This dynamo isn't up to the work," said another. "There's the reason for the delay. The machinery is unsound."

"The machines are in order, I believe," said Snow, who had seen them operate.

The others took it up, and there followed technical talk of the sort Snow liked, though now he listened, chewing his lip, and himself spoke rarely. He had thought to seek the group's opinion of Weber's silence but decided not to, not at this session in any case. And he almost said that he regretted Weber's ever having signed the petition for the writ, using the letters the chaplain had taught him, but you did not say everything to convicts, even those considered friends.

2

Snow delivered on successive Sundays in the prison chapel two sermons with his mind on Weber. In the first he employed a parable of his own invention: a poor son gave his father a poor gift, a handful of seeds, which his rich brother mocked but his wise father gladly accepted. "He planted the seeds and following generations who ate of the fruit that came of this planting blessed the one who had been thus thoughtful." The poorest gift is great in God's sight if it is the best we can afford—his mind on Weber, on having brought the man to the point with what was for him a thinking trust in Christ—the best he could afford—and faith in God's love: seeing Weber working here for a future harvest and serene at the end of that day's work. But now it was not certain.

The next Sunday Snow prayed with his family before breakfast and watched them, feeling remote. He was thrilled by their bright bent heads but made himself remote from them. It did not occur to him that this was like him, that he had been so as a boy. He used to watch his parents and sister, briefly in passionate love, then remove himself from the sense of them, as if he had put them in history, put them beyond everything.

Before that, as a very young boy, he had a knack, which he lost later. He would look his family over and whoever was in the room with him would suddenly begin to grow smaller, though the room remained the same, until they were like toys; they shrank to the size of toy soldiers; it was always his family as far as he could remember, never anyone outside. At first it terrified him, then he liked it, and now it was mixed up in his memory with that child's God. The chronology was uncertain. He thought that by the time he was ten or so he could no longer do it.

Snow walked to the prison looking at the spring day for its gifts, though he did not keep them. The trees rose lightly from the heavy winter; there was a smell of new earth and raw seedlings that maddened him, but for an instant of time only, and then he would render the sensation: what can the minister do and say to make this comprehensible? He could not stay for more than an instant in the thing itself before being swept into the little cycle of passion and distance that had begun when he was ten or so, but in that instant he would be dazzled, blinded by love looming suddenly up: the quickening town, the warden's garden with its roses and tubbed oranges still wrapped in sacks, its dust laid by the dew, the jewels of dew in the web on the gardener's pump and in the grass spiders' tents, the sun blooming in long morning rays like a hand on his back. He turned it all over to God almost at once. His sermon was different from the previous Sunday's—concerned all with love and very little with the intelligent way. It was as if the chaplain were two men in himself, and he was expressing both in this way on the separate occasions.

3

". . . The point is, you see, that David had such great love for his son that he forgave everything. The treachery and conspiracy were forgiven. Do I say 'forgiven'? Why, that's not half of it, men. It was not forgiveness but love the king felt. The father had no choice, don't you know? It was not as if he had conferred with himself: 'Look here, I know this is treachery, and yet it is my own son, and so I forgive him; there is no treacherous act I cannot ultimately forgive since this is my son.' No, sir: not a bit. *There was no choice.* Not either way. He needed to have his sons, and then he had to love them because fathers love their sons, and then he had to weep because children cause their parents to weep. Isn't that true? You have made your parents weep, have you not? And your wives. And you have wept for your children, have you not?

"David went up by the ascent of Mount Olivet and wept, head covered and feet bare, cast out of his kingdom by his son; there on the mount with his household he wept, cursed, or so he supposed, by the Lord. Absalom loved his father and betrayed him, don't you know? Even in the prison of his treachery he loved him. And the father in the prison of his betrayal loved the son, not with his head but with his heart. Absalom was a criminal, understand, and the crime was against his father the king. When Ahithophel said, 'I will smite the king,' the saying pleased Absalom, though he was better counseled at last. There was no excuse for Absalom; no, none. He chose badly, God knows. But in his love *he had no choice!* And no more had his father. When David's armies were strong they went to deal with the treacherous son, but the king commanded, 'Deal gently for my sake with the young man, even with Absalom.'

"Well, you all know what happened, how the boy was killed after all by warlike Joab. 'Deal gently for my sake with the young man.' The righteous are not always gentle, as you know. You made your parents weep. You know you did. You are all here now, every man of you in this prison, for offenses against your State and your God, against your fathers. You have all offended one way or another against men and God, and there is weeping for you and love in spite of it, though we have not, heaven knows . . . we do not deal gently with you. Absalom had no monument, no son of his own, and his father was aware of that. Wasn't it pathetic how Absalom had to put up his own pillar there in the king's dale, a monument to his memory who had no son and could not be king? David *understood.* He understood the offense against him. Our God understands our crimes and our pathetic need to prevail, to be little kings, don't you know? We rear our little stones, but the *great* king is like the sun over all our sad betraying monuments. And we are understood as well; we are loved with gentleness in spite of everything, even if other men, though they be righteous, be not gentle at all. Absalom conspired to assassinate his father the king, and he was loved despite it: don't you see? Well, as I gaze around this sunny hall it is evident to me by your intently listening, your comprehending visages, that you do indeed *see*. I read recognition everywhere. Love. Understanding. You *see*. But now let's put on the brakes. I am not saying—I have not said, you know, that your offenses shall go unpunished, that they may be forgiven without punishment obtaining. They will not. You would not want it even if it were possible, I know. You would be as mad as those poor inmates across the wall if you did not learn to want and then to learn by your punishment. No. You are punished, but you are loved!

"The watchmen came hurrying and said, '*Tidings draw near!*' News was coming to the king, you see: his *Courier-Post,* his *Advertiser* of that long-ago day; and the running of the foremost was like the running of Ahimaaz the son of Zadok. 'Yes? Well, well, all right. Never mind that now. Never mind the victory and all of that. Is the young man Absalom safe?' . . ."

4

Mrs. Snow with her yellow sunshade and the girls in their Sunday outfits of linen and net and their winking white and black boots were a picture. Reverend Snow walked with his hands clasped under his coattails and nodded at people he knew. Everyone was on a bicycle or out on the lake in a boat. The sun had emerged from thickets of cloud, and people on the blinded lake raised their faces to it, then turned away, and the ladies opened their parasols. Behind the bandstand was an oval track for racing bicycles; a shed of horse stalls had been converted into mechanics' quarters and a place for the riders to change or rest. Beyond this at the far shore of the little park bay was the Home for Aged

Men and Couples with spruces dark around it, at the entrance
of which the Belt Line cars, now electrified, stopped to discharge
passengers who would then go into the Home's grounds or into
the park by the same gate. There were picnics on the grass and
fishing from the pier; a few gigs flashed up and down the roadway, horses lifted into a high, strutting, competition trot.

5

Kernahan came from behind the racers' sheds wheeling his
Columbia, looking narrow and self-aware; he had clips on the
ankles of his flannel trousers and wore his shirtsleeves rolled above
the elbow. "How do?" he said to Mrs. Snow, not looking at her;
he ignored the little girls.

"I think you'll be interested to hear our Mr. Weber has broke
his silence at last, Chaplain."

Snow could not have guessed that the news would startle him
so; it made his heart pound, and he had to put his hand on his
coat against it.

"I imagined he was talking in his sleep, then I realize he is
addressing me: What do you think of this, Kernahan? What
about that? And something about his Jenny, the woman that he
killed."

Snow wanted to know the convict's words.

"Ain't I telling you?"

Kernahan swung a leg over the saddle of the bicycle. Crescents
of sweat were on his shirt. "Some I can't repeat in this company,
and you'll guess why. He used your name, not in the complimentary way." Kernahan looked at the young minister, at the
distressed face: these were facts; it was not his fault. Wasn't he
telling him?

"He said, 'Tell Mr. Snow it would not do.'"

"What do you think he meant by it, Corporal?"

"I can't say. He was offering a few items not what you call in the complimentary line, and he threw some cursing into the hopper too." Kernahan was Catholic. It made a difference: he had his shield and his buckler; Snow had his. Snow was a soft man, as much of a woman as a man with his cornsilk hair and bow lips and slim body like a boy's.

"He paced on in his cage simmering-like, then he dropped back onto the bunk, and that was it.

"I thought you would like to hear, Chaplain, because you was so often urging him to speak and he would not."

Kernahan's bicycle wavered over the path, the man's back straight, knees held in tight, pedaling with the toe tips; his head was high and it turned from side to side of the path as he went.

6

At eight in the morning after the barber had gone Kernahan would bring a basin of warm water, soap, and a rough towel and watch him wash. Then there was breakfast. If Weber wanted to use the bucket, Kernahan strolled back into his cubicle beside the death room. McDade came on. If Mrs. Buxton was going to visit, she was gone by half past eleven.

At twelve or so, when the prisoner was willing, he was permitted a walk in the large room in which the cages stood, exercising that way, while McDade watched from his chair, tapping the heavy stick against his hand. This was a man, after all. McDade was not Kernahan, and he liked Weber. He could not help liking a man. In the early days Weber would not take any exercise. But during the time Snow was preparing him for baptism he began a bit: walking up and down in the big room, performing calisthenics; he would look at the high window, inhale through flared nostrils, and thump his chest with his fists; like a man with a future, McDade thought. It had been good to see that. And his appetite had been excellent at the time too.

Weber's food was better than the messroom's. His bootleg was drinkable and had plenty of sugar and real cream in it; he was permitted cocoa, or tea if he preferred, and some days the man would switch off, choosing with a frown, as if it mattered. For breakfast he had not only the oatmeal porridge or potato hash given the rest of the prison but an egg too, boiled in the shell, and fresh butter, and all the toasted bread he could eat. His midday meal and supper were served half an hour later than the messroom's. He was allowed meat or fish three and sometimes four times a week—ham, hake, chicken, stew—first-rate menu, better than the keeper's at home where meat once a week was all they could afford. In the middle of the morning or afternoon, if he was hungry and wished it, Weber was served with molasses and bread and bootleg, which was the prison name for coffee. McDade had never seen a condemned man gain weight. At first Weber had eaten heartily; now for almost two weeks he had eaten little; but he looked about the same to the keeper, neither fatter nor thinner than the day he came in over a year ago.

In the afternoon Principal Keeper Keough would come, sometimes in company with Warden Buxton, more often alone. He was small and wore old-fashioned mutton-chop side whiskers and a uniform as neat as a sailor's, his cap cocked just slightly to one side of his head so that he had an air. His glance was quick and secret like the prisoners'. He would bring along Weber's ration of tobacco and pass it over with a kind of ceremony, keeping his eyes on the other man's chest. It made McDade smile: Major Keough, a prisoner himself in most of his gestures, secretly tucking the bit of tobacco into the man's palm, avoiding his eyes. "You silly old coconut," thought McDade, amused. Weber had not smoked either in ten days.

On the Saturday afternoon before he spoke for the first time since his silence began, Weber accepted Keough's tobacco, rolled four cigarettes with the papers he kept in his shirt pocket, and smoked them one after the other, taking his lights from McDade.

And when the day watch brought in his supper, saying, "They've given you the white soup and salt horse for tomorrow's dinner tonight, Weber," he could tell that the convict was on the edge of speech, like a clock winding to strike, though he did not speak just then.

He began past midnight, with Kernahan on again, having paced regularly up and down inside his cage since lights-out.

7

"Are you asleep, Kernahan?"

The keeper replied, "No, I'm not."

Weber gave a little gasp of husky laughter. "I'll tell them you were and get you the sack." His voice was harsh. He kept clearing his throat. When he spoke it was slowly.

"Well, shall I tell you what I think?"

"Suit yourself."

"There's no end to it, no conclusion. It's uncertain, that's what I think. I'll tell it to that little man, the parson," he said slowly in his rusty voice. "It won't do. It did not do. I could see it wasn't going to. But here it is: I can't see what will."

Kernahan asked, interested, "Why have you been quiet, Weber?"

The other did not appear to have heard.

"Do you know you haven't spoke in ten days?"

Weber kept clearing his throat. At length he said, "Yes." And then: "What do you think of that application on the cruel and unusual—won't it be denied?"

"Everyone agrees it will be."

"P'r'aps it will be," the man said calmly. "How do you think I was doing on that day before I knew? How did I look—like a man?"

"You looked all right, Weber. You didn't look like you was afraid."

"Yes. Well, it won't do. Tell that to that little cock, if you please. And to the woman. I am not here to play a game before people. Tell him that and tell that damned woman not to come to me here."

He went on for an hour, sometimes stopping, but then picking up again. He fell asleep with roosters going off around the prison, missed the 7:30 bell, and had to be awakened for breakfast.

8

"I hear you are addressing the throngs, Rupert," Warden Buxton said.

"I'm not saying much, though."

"That's always wise."

Buxton stood outside of the cage, tired and serious, the little principal keeper a deferential step behind him.

"My wife will want to have a word with you, I'm sure, perhaps tomorrow morning. She is pleased to hear that you are yourself again." He made a gesture, showing Weber his palms to indicate the openness among them.

"I don't want her."

"Major Keough has brought tobacco. Do you want that?"

Weber, his back to them, nodded slightly.

McDade opened the cage and Keough started to enter, but Weber surprised them by turning and walking out of the cage between the two keepers, his shoulder brushing Keough. The three authorities were taken aback and could not act for a moment; then Buxton said, "Where do you think you are going, Rupert?"

"To have my walk."

He had paused outside of the cage, arms hanging. He stared down at the floor.

"Not now, Weber," McDade said. "It isn't the time for that."

He moved slightly toward the convict, swinging the lead-loaded stick from its thong, and Keough had raised the cane he carried. Without glancing up, Weber returned to the cage. Keough handed over the tobacco in his secretive way, and at once Weber sat down on his bunk, and began to roll a cigarette, ignoring them.

"By the way," Buxton said, "you may be having company. We will probably transfer a man named Fisch here from Sing Sing. He has been convicted of murder."

"Will they kill him with the electricity?"

"Well," said Buxton, "that's the law now."

"But I'll be first?"

"There is your stay, as you know, to permit application for what they style a writ of error to the United States Supreme Court."

"But that don't wash, does it?"

"We can't say as to that." He underlined the slang: "It may very well wash."

"It won't."

There was silence. Weber sat on his bunk smoking. The others stood just outside, McDade and Keough alert, though the principal keeper was looking the other way, Buxton flushed and anxious. Weber's excursion outside of his cage into their midst uninvited had startled them. It made him for a moment what they knew he had been all along but somehow forgotten: a danger. He had murdered someone, after all.

Buxton said later to Clark, the doctor, "It put things into perspective. To see that—almost as if he would attack us; it made me . . ." He laughed slightly. "It made me feel better! I wish they would show spirit. But in their cages they become lambs."

The warden had business in New York. He would return by Albany and hand in his monthly report at the State House. He and Clark were having a drink while Buxton waited for his train.

"I wish we were finished with him," said the doctor.

"Mrs. Buxton is deeply concerned. She is nearly past reasoning with."

Clark, after looking thoughtful, said, "In any case he appears to have regained the faculty of speech and is using it." And, when Buxton said nothing: "You *would* like to be out of it, I guess."

"I've never liked it. I never wanted to be the first. I wish to heaven someone else could be first in this damnable business. It is killing Mrs. Buxton. And the electric light companies are only using the poor wretch and his fate as a means to fight each other. My own duties are by now entirely obscured."

A reporter called on Buxton in New York. They sat in armchairs in the lobby of his hotel. "I have never liked it," Buxton said, worn out by his train journey, still alarmed and anxious. "Don't suggest that I am influenced in this, but I was glad to see the most recent delay since it gives me a chance to make certain of my machinery." In answer to a question: "I cannot believe that it is the intention of the new execution law to help Mr. Edison out in his rivalry with Mr. Westinghouse. I cannot believe it is the new law's purpose to give you people—not to single out the *Journal*—an opportunity to sell newspapers with the sort of publicity that is certain to hinder my work, the work of our laws and courts. Yet here you see these things going on, don't you? My duty has been thwarted and obscured by this kind of thing for months, and I am tired of it."

And in reply to another question: "I am here on business to do with Clarkville Prison's manufacturing interests, which are still operating at an alarming deficit. Now, why don't you ask about that? There is no circulation in that, I suppose. I have still five hundred men idle in my jurisdiction for want of what I consider suitable industries. Morale is poor. The death rate is up, and there has been an unequaled numerical incidence of insanity— all due to idleness: a situation that is barely eased under the new and, I feel, inadequate laws regulating prison management and labor. Why doesn't the *Journal* ask us about that?"

He ought not to lose his temper or take the press into his confidence, but he was tired and anxious, more so than he had been since Weber first was committed to his charge. The gesture, that violent step outside of the cage without permission, had thrown everything into the light again. In one sense it made him feel better, as any show of spirit did; but finally it alarmed him, put all of the old questions up to him again. He liked very little of it; it was harming Mrs. Buxton. He did not want to be the first man to do this.

The lawyer, Marcus Bush, who obtained the most recent writ and personally conveyed it to Buxton at Clarkville, called on him. "How is my client?"

"Physically all right."

"Yes, there is a rumor that he has lost his mind."

"I didn't mean that. He is just the same as he has always been."

"Well," the lawyer said, "that's too bad, Hiram, because you know there is no chance that the application will be accepted."

"Then why did you make the application?"

"I may leave no stone unturned in my effort to save this man from being killed with the alternating current."

"George Westinghouse does not want it."

"Certainly he does not want it. Do you blame him?"

Later Bush said, not smiling, "Why, I suggest that he lose his mind indeed. I am amazed that he has not done so already. Any ordinary man would have. I would have. My own next move will be to attempt to replevin the electrical apparatus up there—the dynamos and switches and so on that are stamped with the company's name; but that I can tell you will be futile too."

In Albany Buxton visited electrician Stone's little laboratory that was set up in the basement of his house. It had the same odor he noticed in the prison death room when they ran an experiment. "I want you to come up again to Clarkville soon and go over our dynamo and the other apparatus."

"It was in good order as left," the electrician replied in an irritated way. "Will the application be denied then?"

Buxton told him what Marcus Bush had said: "It would ask

the U.S. Supreme Court to consider that the highest court of our State denied Weber due process; it is unlikely to be allowed."

"The machinery is all right, Warden. It will kill him instantaneously." He did not approve of Buxton's consulting with Weber's lawyer, whom he considered merely as Westinghouse's. "Here is this Cardew meter, which I've gone over and which now functions as it should. You might as well put it into your bag and take it along to the prison. When the application is denied and you've picked a new date I'll come up and go over everything, and we'll wire in the meter then. We can do another calf or dog to be certain, but if it's after June 1st you understand I won't do the actual execution; my contract is up then. This is not my idea of a lark, I assure you. It's made me nervous, the whole thing, and I want to be rid of it."

He said at the door, "We killed some dogs last week over at Orange, New Jersey, with a very few volts of alternating: 200, 250. It went quick as lightning each time."

9

"Are you cold?"

"Oh, no, I ain't," the convict replied with what the chaplain supposed was irony. He wore all the clothing he was permitted to keep in his cage: his round woolen cap with its gray and black bands, his knitted waistcoat, and the horizontal-striped winter overcoat with its tick lining and the white good-behavior bull's-eye on its shoulder, which he had put on over the short jacket that he habitually wore. His back was to the other.

"Can't you tell me what you meant?" Snow asked again.

"That's what I meant."

He made a gesture at the illustrated Bible and Common Prayer on the table.

"How wouldn't it do?"

The little look of irony lingered.

"Won't you tell me, Rupert? It has done until now, I supposed."
He had been about to suggest a prayer, but because he felt the
risk of pressing him he did not. "All right. Let's sit here for a
time."

Then Weber said something.

"I didn't get that, brother."

Weber said, turning and looking shyly at the chaplain, "It
didn't go, and I don't know what will if that don't."

"Well, I think it will go, brother," Snow was unable to resist
saying, "if I understand what you mean by the word."

The prisoner rose and shouted, "Didn't I just now say it won't!"
Snow rose too. McDade had come to the door of his cubicle.

"All right, Weber," the keeper said. He opened the cage without waiting for the chaplain's signal, and as he had earlier Weber
stepped forward toward the door, moving ahead of the minister
as if he would escape from the cage. McDade, alert now,
blocked him. "Let Mr. Snow pass, Weber."

The prisoner backed up. He sat on the bunk, bulky in his
clothing. Snow looked in from the outside, and Weber grew
smaller and smaller, moving away rapidly as if down a tunnel; he
was going swiftly right away from him down a long dim-lighted
passage, rocking slightly as if he were on one of those handcars
rail gangs used. Though everything around him retained its usual
proportion, Weber himself, retreating at a giddy speed, grew
smaller until he appeared to be no bigger than Snow's hand, and
there he stayed: a Tom Thumb.

10

McDade stood beside her, watchful, until she said, "Go on
back, Fred. We're all right. How are you feeling, Rupert? It isn't
a nice day at all."

"No, it ain't."

He would not look at her, but he had spoken. She had been

reading to him during the last days of his silence from a sermon entitled *The Prison-House.* The marker she took from the book was of embroidered silk: Niagara Falls, Ontario. "May I read?"

He shook his head.

Then they would talk for a bit, as they used to do: "All right, Rupert?" But she was tired, as if waiting for the man to speak had exhausted her, and looked longingly at the book in her hand. Painfully, she cast about in her mind.

"What would you think if I told you that dear old Clarkville is no longer ours to call dear or not? At least that *may* be the case, Rupert, as my husband was telling me that a certain lady in Indiana claims to be the heir of the old Van Kaamp estate, and that is most of the city within its present boundaries. It includes the prison land too. Wouldn't that put our city fathers in a pickle? We would all be paying rent to the Indiana lady, I suppose. . . ."

He shook his head, not looking at her.

"I believe she's only spinning a yarn, looking out for her own gain," she said.

She had been to Ithaca to the opera a few days before, and the college students were rowdy. But it made Mrs. Buxton smile. "They were all upstairs and sang 'Annie Rooney' during the interval. They were awful," she said smiling.

The convict said in a childish way, "I don't want you."

Mrs. Buxton said, "I must go. I have very much enjoyed this. I was delighted . . ." She did not know how to finish.

She had visited prisoners for ten years. Twice before she had visited the condemned, and the sentences of both had been commuted to life imprisonment, as if the events of her visits and the commutations were related. But now she thought that she was too tired to be of use. Something imminent slept coiled in her; she could not help Weber. Later, remembering this morning and her thoughts, she said to herself: "I am irrational." The sun had not been out. The cage was dark as a sewer, the man in it yellow against the dark mesh of the cage, a knee clasped in his hands, breath scarcely evident; he spoke a few words, it was true, but that was nothing after all. She was exhausted past the repair of sleep or distraction. "I am only forty-nine," she thought irrationally. Yellowish, a shadow in his cage, the man was as distant now as when he had been silent. Ought she to touch him? His end lay inside her, using her, and she could not help it.

11

Snow said with great earnestness, "I am talking about love, and you know that God loves you. Don't you know that when He chooses this is how, invariably, He chooses? You may suppose I'm merely talking of things as I want them—'soft,' you think. Not at all: nothing to do with my wishes or yours; nothing to be achieved by petition and prayer, attention to duty, as if we were aldermen meeting or citizens in church. You may petition much with more or less success but not God's love for you: that is sure!

"Why do you imagine our Lord gave his life away for us? What is behind that, do you imagine? Brother, haven't we been over this time and again? Now listen: men were in terrible difficulties then, exactly as you were before your baptism, and as you would appear to be now, though in fact it is merely your psychology, not your spiritual state, which has been affected by this delay in your going home. . . .

"'I pity you,' says the Father: 'I pity you! I love you and am up here waiting for you! I am so lonely for you, awaiting you here—for you to come safe home!'"

12

"Yes! I too! Yes, indeed! Bank on it!"

"And McDade too, I guess," retorted Weber with thick irony.

"Sergeant McDade as well," Snow said. "Certainly! We pity you and we love you! Not that ours is a patch on God's."

Weber said, "No." And then: "It don't go down with me."

The convicted man grew as small as Tom Thumb. This had not happened to Snow since he was ten or eleven years old, and here it had happened twice in two days, making him dizzy and ill, so that he had to rap hard on the cage wall and get McDade to let him out.

three

The Application Is Denied

1

Keough and McDade put Weber into a closed hack at the farm garden entrance of the prison and drove in it the long way around under the tremendous walls to the railroad station, which was opposite the prison entrance; there they met Warden Buxton and Weber's lawyer. A few correspondents stood farther along the platform; Buxton had asked them to keep their distance.

Bush greeted his client. "How are you?"

"I guess I'm all right."

"Just enjoy your holiday. There's nothing to it."

"I know."

Weber stood, his right hand chained to McDade's left, up against a baggage van piled high with bandboxes and bags and Russia-leather valises.

Bush said aside to Buxton, "How do you think he'll do?"

"He may arouse some emotion."

"But what sort?" Bush looked humorous, his sharp dark eyes

going over his client. He hoped he would not regret asking the judges to allow Weber's presence. "You see?"

2

Weber had a glimpse of the town from the platform. There was Empire Street in the early morning, and the Clark House with big trees only stopping for the cross street and the Canal bridge going in a ragged leafy line down to it. And there was the prison from the outside. A few convict safeties were working up close to the main gate on the inside to get a glimpse of Weber, brooms and rakes going, and there were civilian faces at the administration windows. Even the screws way up in the corner gun emplacements were doing their best to see him. Weber had a good look around too. He could do a few letters by now, and anybody knew the billboards: "Pillsbury's Best" over the railroad bridge.

Keough wore a pistol in a holster under his coat and kept a step behind McDade and the prisoner. They followed Buxton and the lawyer into the station building where a crowd of early passengers waited; Weber did not look at them. To even things up there was the Royal Baking Powder advertisement, which he recognized by its picture. The floors were scrubbed, there were heavy white spittoons here and there; he liked a station waiting room.

Someone said, "Good luck to you, Weber."

Bush sat on a bench, opened his briefcase, and began taking papers out of it. They led Weber through a door into the depot master's office. From there he could see past the ticket-seller on his high stool through the brass wicket back out to the waiting room. A man in a good-looking pearl-gray derby asked for a round trip to Rochester. He appeared to be staring through at the convict, but Weber could not be certain; he did not care. There was a dog back here, a sort of collie, curled up under the ticket man's table gazing at Weber, its tail beating gently. He looked at the dog with attention but only briefly. The ticket man wore polished boots with elastic sides; he had them hooked up on the rungs of the stool, their toes tapping the air as he worked: good shoes. Everything was well set up back here in this private place. Long schedules and excursion offers hung from spikes; there were the black typewriters and telegraph machines, and a couple of yellow brass telephones gleaming; tickets stood up in vertical bins like the coins did in racks in banks. The ticket man kept glancing back at him, but his swift white hands continued to write and stamp and tear tickets, take the green bills and make change. Buxton stood near the window looking out on the tracks; when one or another of the correspondents pacing the platform tried to look in he saw only the warden. The depot master hovered nearby, pretending he had business here. McDade seemed as calm as a hill beside him. They all remained standing: Weber, McDade, Keough, Buxton.

The prisoner wore the clothes he had turned in when he was committed: the good King suit, his checked cap, and boots; they had even turned back to him his old watch with the silver chain and his calf wallet. He had kept hidden under a secret flap in the wallet a lifelike and detailed pen sketch of a naked couple going at it, the man just lowering himself onto the woman, she lolling back looking half asleep, legs apart . . . lying there to be sketched like that! His heart jumped when he found the wallet in the jacket, but the sketch, which he had won in a game at Denny O'Brien's in Philly, was gone, the secret pocket empty as air. And then he realized that he did not care. It would do him no good any more, and he did not care about the confiscation of the sketch.

A train came in making its explosive noise and blowing steam; Buxton started nervously for the door, but the depot master told them it was not theirs. Its unaccustomed noise so close hurt Weber's ears and rattled him, as the motion of the hack coming around the prison had made him queasy; he was not used to sounds or motion after the still water of the prison basement and his silence.

When their train arrived they escorted Weber out through the depot master's own parlor and kitchen, where a woman stared at him open-mouthed, to an exit onto the stones and sleepers beyond the end of the platform; then they walked along to the mail and baggage cars. Weber could see passengers climbing up to their cars far away at the other end: a lady raising a knee high in her long skirt; he saw a man with a little boy, the trainman looking at his watch.

Keough advised Buxton to keep the prisoner in the baggage car, but it did not look comfortable enough to the warden, and he went forward to see if he could not find a car that would serve. Weber waited among the barrels and crates. There was a closed spicy odor of wood, coal oil, and leather. They remained standing as they had before, and then, when the warden returned and beckoned, followed him, jostling each other and bracing awkwardly against the motion of the train. Buxton had arranged to have the last passenger car emptied. They sat on the left facing front so that Weber was against the window, and McDade, with his right arm free, was on the aisle. Major Keough had turned the back rest of the next seat, and he and the warden sat facing them, Keough with his neat little knees against the convict's; Buxton read an Albany newspaper. Weber looked out of the window at the farmland they passed through.

3

IN RE WEBER.
Opinion of the Court.
. . . that, contrary to the constitutions of the State of New York and of the United States, and contrary to his objection and exception, duly and timely taken in due form of law, he was sentenced to undergo a cruel and unusual punishment, as appears by a copy of the pretended judgment, warrant or mandate hereto annexed and made a

part of this petition and marked Exhibit "A" by virtue of which such imprisonment or restraint is claimed to be made; that he is deprived of liberty and threatened with deprivation of life without due process of law, contrary to the constitutions of New York and of the United States, and contrary to his objection and exception thereto, duly and timely taken. The imprisonment is stated to be illegal because it is contrary to the provisions of each of said constitutions.

We have read with much interest . . .

In *Wilkerson v. Utah*, 99 U.S. 130, 135 . . . Punishments are cruel when they involve torture or a lingering death; but the punishment of death is not cruel, within the meaning of that word as used in the Constitution. It implies there something inhuman and barbarous, something more than the mere extinguishment of life. . . .

4

Opinion of the Court . . .

The courts of New York held that the mode adopted in this instance might be said to be unusual because it was new, but that it could not be assumed to be cruel in the light of that common knowledge which has stamped certain punishments as such; that it was for the legislature to say in what manner sentence of death should be executed; that this act was passed in the effort to devise a more humane method of reaching the result; that the courts were bound to presume that the legislature was possessed of the facts upon which it took action; and that by evidence taken *aliunde* the statute that presumption could not be overthrown. They went further, and expressed the opinion that upon the evidence the legislature had attained by the act the object had in view in its passage.

The decision of the state courts sustaining the validity of the act under the state constitution is not reëxaminable here, nor was that decision against any title, right, privilege, or immunity specially set up or claimed by the petitioner under the Constitution of the United States.

Treating it as involving an adjudication that the statute was not repugnant to the Federal Constitution, that conclusion was so plainly right that we should not be justified in allowing the writ upon the ground that error might have supervened therein. . . .

The application for a writ of error is   *Denied*

Both Fox and Grace of the State commission that had put through the new technique came at the Governor's request to hear the court's decision and, when Weber's application was denied, went home together as far as Albany, where Fox changed trains for New York and Grace for Saratoga Springs.

"We have a clear course now."

"I think so," Dr. Fox replied in his pedantic style, "but the delays have been cruel to the man, and the publicity has put the new law in a poor light."

Fox was slightly awkward in the presence of the other, even though Grace's manner was kind. At the electrical execution hearings in the previous summer the referee had had to summon Grace by telegraph sent to his yacht, which was cruising the Maine coast, and Grace had come along on the third day, comfortable, self-possessed, "knowing his apples," as a reporter put it, called Edison by his first name at the sessions, while the Wizard called him "Commodore," and measured swords fearlessly with Westinghouse's man. ("We all know that the law is the only exact profession, Mr. Bush.") It was Fox who, with Governor Hill's warm assent, had nominated Grace chairman of the Commission on Capital Punishment two years before, both men recognizing the value of a famous and respected name in the matter. Neither had been disappointed. Conrad Grace carried the matter forward with vigor. The bill was put into law almost at once. He spoke learnedly on his new subject and turned out articles for *Scribner's* and *The North American Review,* in one of which he coined the word *electrolethe* to describe the new method. If Dr. Fox was the father of electrical execution, as the correspondents called him, Grace, in the doctor's view and by his own metaphor, was its obstetrician.

"I've heard a report that Weber is pretending to be mad."

Fox was anxious on the point.

"Well," Grace said with a little sideways smile at his companion, "if he is as normal as some we've run into in this, they may have a case."

The medical man tried to engage Grace in a conversation about sailing, which he had been reading up on, and Grace said, "We had a good day last week."

"Steady wind from the southwest, wasn't it?"

The other appeared to be surprised.

"I follow yachting news."

Fox did not address Grace by name. They were of an age, and he would not say "mister"; "Conrad" was permanently out of the question, Fox knew; he did not like to call any man by his last name alone, though it was the custom today among equals. So far he had solved the problem by avoiding it, but he was about to try something.

"The *Cormorant* is a class three?"

Grace was surprised, apparently pleased.

"I recall that you did your course in just over four hours, forty minutes, Commodore, which placed you second. Now, that is no mean accomplishment considering the competition."

"First in our class would have made it a greater one."

Dr. Fox was intent upon how the "Commodore" had gone down; he used it again after a time, and it seemed both correct and natural.

6

There were telegrams at Fox's house in New York. His oldest friend, who, when he was a senator, presented the resolution to appoint the Commission, wired: CONGRATULATIONS ON YOUR NOBLE WORK. SLOW JUSTICE COMES ABREAST HUMANITY. Governor Hill sent thanking him for time taken from his regular duties to see to this "irksome" civic one—a rambling costly message, of which Fox did not doubt Grace had received a twin. Dr. Nerney, who was to supervise the autopsy on the electrically executed man, had left his card, as had the Attorney General and Slocum, the Erie County district attorney. Nerney came by again next morning, and he and Fox sat in the front parlor of the Seventy-second Street brownstone.

Nine years before, Nerney performed the post-mortem on one of the first men to be killed by an accidental contact with the alternating current dynamo.

"Did you see the joke in the Clarkville paper?"

Fox had not and did not understand it when Nerney told it. ". . . dy-na-mo: *die-no-more*?"

"Will you help us out?" Nerney asked later.

"I want my attention for the machinery and Weber's reactions at the instant of contact. I will watch you cut him up and take the notes of your commentary, if you like."

Nerney said, "You know nerve tissue was burned away in the case of Goodwin"—referring to the accidental death of 1881—"and flesh too. I've been thinking we'd better not burn the man's flesh or the reporters will get after us."

"It's a matter of the contacts being exactly applied."

Mrs. Fox looked into the parlor. There were patients in the dispensary who had been waiting for an hour: "Meek as lambs," she said.

"I'm certain anyhow that death will be instant. I expect a pronounced rigor," said Nerney. "What interests me chiefly is how the shock will work on the nerve tissues and the effect on the blood. Blood changes will interest me a good deal. I don't concern myself so much with the effect on capillary tissue."

Mrs. Fox went away.

"I am solely interested in the machinery and in the initial response. I expect that all of our hopes will be satisfied," said Fox.

Nerney went on about Goodwin for a time and then said, "You are like the bridegroom, Fox. You have your heart's desire, are confident of it, and yet can't help a bit of stage fright."

To a reporter who called on the telephone the same evening

Fox, still irritated by Nerney's words, said, "I am convinced that death will be instantaneous. . . . No danger that the current will be kept on long enough to burn his body. I anticipate no disfigurement. Every effort will be made to secure a positive contact. I would like to have him talking, addressing the witnesses, when the current is turned on, for then the attendants could have an opportunity to see how quickly death would follow an electrical shock such as Weber will receive."

7

Mrs. Fox kept a scrapbook and spent an hour after supper pasting the telegrams and news reports into it, while her husband watched from the other side of the cold fireplace.

"The Senator's message is in blank verse," she said smiling. She read it aloud, beating time. She said, "It is too bad that Mr. Grace does not live in New York. Then you could see your new friend more often."

Having heard her husband's way of referring to Grace, she asked at first, "Do *you* call him that?"

"Those who know him give Mr. Grace that unofficial title. There's nothing in it. The fact is that he is an associate, not a friend in the sense you mean."

8

In Albany electrician Stone gave an interview to the *New York Times.*

"Unless Buxton fixes a date within the next week or ten days I am out of it," Stone offered at once, "and you may write in your paper that I am delighted to be out of it. You could say 'tickled pink.' That isn't your high journalistic style, is it?—though it describes the emotion. A man named Taggart will take over from me, I think. I will check the equipment at Clarkville once more, and that's all." They walked in a park near the electrician's house. Stone was tall and skinny, and he raced in a nervous manner along the park paths, making abrupt turns, so that Chaney, the *Times* man, who was tall himself, had to trot to keep up.

"For two years—since this month in '88 when I first published— I have been under attack, and Mr. Thomas A. Edison, who was good enough to let me make my tests in his magnificent electrical laboratory, has been under attack. His enemies have not forgiven him for that kindness to me. I proved the continuous current safe if my apparatus is employed, and that alternating produces instant and painless death at low pressures. Let's make it clear that I undertook this for the purpose of protecting life, and that due only to the expert knowledge I had gained of death-currents . . .

". . . extremely reluctant . . ."

He rubbed his hair so that it stood in thin flames on his scalp. He and the reporter had paused beside a pond choked with lily pads, and there they lingered, small under the big trees, Stone hunched crane-like, Chaney smoothing his mustache and scribbling notes, a long spatted shoe up on a bench, the saps and powders of spring floating around them.

". . . knowing that it would subject me to abuse, but I was persuaded that this application of what Mr. Westinghouse falsely terms a safe and harmless current would educate the people to handle it with caution and save many lives. I at first *declined* to assume responsibility of designing a machine for experiment with human life, then later, for the reasons I've named, agreed, and selected the selfsame Westinghouse dynamo which has killed so many innocent people who made accidental contact with its deadly wires in the few years since its introduction to commercial use.

". . . banish it from the streets and buildings, thus ending the terrible, needless slaughter of unoffending men . . .

"Through a third party. Westinghouse would not sell me a dynamo.

"Write it all down if you like. I am past caring. Here, let me tell you something you cannot write down to illustrate the degree to which my nerves have been affected by these articles attacking my purpose."

Chaney put his notebook and pencil into a pocket and, like a fighter who wants to show that he is peaceful, opened his hands. When he had heard, he thought to himself: "It will be the death of me. I will die."

9

Mariage.

Jimmy Duff, the theatrical manager, was a friend of Chaney's; so was Solomon, the composer of operettas. Duff's company was going to put on a piece by Messrs. Stephens and Solomon at the Palmer in August, *The Red Hussar,* and he was bringing over Marie Tempest to sing Kitty. Chaney, who knew everyone, knew her.

He and Duff and Solomon were drunk in Sloan's on Third Avenue. Solomon did his party turn at the upright. He sat on the bench facing away from the piano, then leaned back, got his head under the keyboard, crossed his hands, and played marches upside down. Chaney sat bigger than life, red and grinning, "exhaling disaster," as Solomon said of him. "Did you read the one in the *Gazette?*" He was, for Chaney, drunk.

" '*I'm a-goin' ohm to dynamo, Rupert Weber says.*'

"Die-no-more," he explained.

He repeated what Stone had told him in confidence, having written it down on the train from Albany so as not to forget the exact words, which would have been a pity: " 'I have been unable to do the spring planting—you follow me? I cannot stand up to *mariage* with Mrs. Stone, have been unable to for nearly half a year so affected are my nerves,' " he read from his notebook.

They wept with laughter.

"He asked me not to write it in the *New York Times.*"

They fell off their chairs, pleading with him.

"He said that?"

"How did he look?"

"Oh, please!"

"*Mariage!*"

Chaney said to them later, seriously, "Yes, he's Edison's man, though I can't publish that. I think he's supposed to put over the continuous current, make it sell, since Edison's trade in it is not brisk and Westinghouse's in the other is. *Entre nous,* as we are officially behind the Wizard."

"Well, they'll kill him now, won't they?"

"That's it. And the only thing left for the Westinghouse people would be if the rig there at Clarkville didn't work too well."

The composer looked a little queer at the notion, and even Duff, who was a cheerful man, blinked solemnly; but after a moment he began to pound his knee. "*Mariage!*" he shouted, which was all that was needed to set them off again.

10

A life-size darky with electric clockwork insides lifted its arm in greeting at the door of the theater, and its popeyes rolled and lit each time it did. The Edison Paris exhibition had been brought over to New York and installed in the Lenox Lyceum. There were telephone and phonograph displays, and a miniature electric railroad with a mile of tracks. A telephone system had been connected to the Broadway Theater, and by means of amplified sound everyone at the Lyceum could hear a performance of *The Mikado* in progress—not that it was quiet enough for a minute to hear. The electrician Taggart, who was to take Stone's place at Clarkville, was scornful of it all yet would not leave. A doll recited prayers, and Mrs. Taggart nearly wept—all P. T. Barnum nonsense; yet when his wife asked to go, saying it was too hot, using her satin fan, and closing her eyes to show she was tired, he would not leave but went irritably along from exhibit to exhibit, twisting the ends of his mustache, punching buttons and pulling levers to see what the gadgets would do and working out how they did it. To his satisfaction he saw that a featured demonstration—a performance entitled "A Peep into the Twentieth Century"—was not in operation and that what they called the "theatorium," in which it was to be housed, was shut, its gold-tasseled curtain drawn.

Later they walked down Broadway to save the hack, and he told his wife that probably he would be in charge of the machinery at the State Prison. It was supposed to be good news, but she said, "I wish you would not."

He told her that it was necessary work. If he didn't do it, someone else would.

She searched for a way to phrase her question. She asked at last, "Will you have to watch him?"

"See him die? Yes, no way around that if I'm in charge."

11

Stone was put on the rear porch to wait. After a while a boy came through a gap in the tall hedge at the bottom of the lawn carrying a scabby Spanish cat. He looked directly up at him, and Stone made a gesture to wave him away, but the boy started up the long slope. Childs, an Edison assistant, returned and said, "That's all right, then."

"I want to make my position clear to him."

"Mr. Edison says it's of no consequence if you are sure you

47

can't continue, though of course he would rather have you see it through."

Stone said, "I want to suit him, naturally. It's just that I can't manage. I must quit. It's a question of my health."

"Only, when you go up again be certain everything is running smoothly. . . . Look, there's another one." He shouted, "No!" cupping his hands around his mouth. *"No more cats!* We don't want any more!" He flapped his arms, the gray laboratory coat flying around him, and the boy stopped.

"They don't know we're through in that line."

They had been buying cats and dogs for a dollar or so each to test the effects of alternating and direct currents in execution, and boys still came to sell strays.

"So he won't see me," Stone said, defeated.

"He understands your position. If you're unwell and can't stay on the job . . ."

The boy turned and started back down the slope, and Stone left.

12

The Buffalo *Star-Union* offered McDade a dinner in the Clark House on his day off, but the keeper declined. He would feel out of place and uncomfortable, not that he wasn't as good a man as the men who patronized the public rooms there. He suggested instead a saloon not far from his own house where they could eat a first-class bar lunch and drink good beer.

"Why, we were holding him out in the corridor, you know, while the hearing went on because the lawyer decided he'd make a poor impression after all. When Mr. Buxton came out of the courtroom to tell him the word, that his application had been denied, he just looked steady at him. He didn't say anything at that moment." McDade drank his beer in long swallows, touching the back of his big hand to his mustache each time he did. "Let me try to remember." It was not much for the press.

He would like to please this reporter, but there was no end to what they wanted. He had trouble recalling Weber's statements, few as they were, but that was what these people demanded: word for word what the man had said. He supposed Kernahan did better at it. He also supposed Kernahan took money, which he would not; a beer, like this, and a sandwich perhaps.

He would drop it all, all the jailhouse life, he thought, if he were not so old. He ought to be back of a horse's tail with the handles of a plow in his hands like his father had been and his brothers, working the land of the rich lake shores, or helping along with the big city projects: the sewers, and roadbed work, and public construction. That was the kind of thing.

"A man doesn't show much, you know," he said. "You can't get a great deal out of just a few words or a man's expression. I've seen others waiting. Here and over at Clinton where I was posted before. Now there was a fuss when Weber quit speaking for a time, but I've known men to suddenly start a silence, a long one, men outside of the condemned cells as well as in. Men go into the jail here, which is what we call our punishment cells on the north wall, and come out silent, and stay that way for weeks. They look around them quietly all day, like they're amazed by it all; it's all new to them. I see them touch things the way you'd pick up a kitten, do everything slowly. It's as if they have come back from the dead, which in a way . . .

"I'll tell you: the jails are terrible places, really. It's true that things go on there."

He was getting old. All the screws knew without being told that there were certain occurrences they did not talk about on the outside; not that this young fellow would want to get him into trouble. Two ounces of bread and a gill of water a day in those black cells that had no furniture, so that the poor men had to stand or lie on the floor and water running over it half the time, in their own stinks; and the rats; and if the screws did not take them out at odd hours of the night at their whim and administer beatings, McDade did not know much. The *Star-Union* spoke nothing beyond a brief question now and then, just jotted a note and drank his beer. That was shorthand, McDade supposed; he was nearsighted. The trouble was that since Weber's time at Clarkville the keeper had talked to too many reporters and as a result had grown careless. He thought: why not be out there on South Line Street each morning with a shovel and pick or wheelbarrow and a few old friends working at your side?—instead of living back in that darkness where in a little time, now that the application was denied, he would have to help deprive a poor wretch of his only life—a young fellow in health, no different from this reporter, and strong as a tree. He did not suppose that girl Weber had knocked in the head when he was drunk was better than she should have been; he was not condoning it; God forbid.

"You don't want to get into trouble with the law, young man," said McDade heavily.

It was a warm day, and he took more than he was accustomed to drink. He had seen the vengeance of the law, what they called the satisfaction of its outraged majesty. He had seen a man take fifteen minutes to die at the end of a rope while the witnesses—important men: doctors, parsons—fainted like women; and he did not suppose for an instant that this new notion of burning a man to death by tying him into an electrical circuit was going to be better.

"I'll tell you what I think is in Weber's mind so far as I can make out."

Well, he had better not.

He put a heavy hand on the young man's arm. "You're all right. You seem to be a good fellow. . . ."

The Bible was cunning. Never mind about the devil quoting from it; it was cunning all on its own. The Lord did not kill Cain for his crime. He cast him out, a fugitive. He was a vagabond from then on. If he went out to farm, then the earth would not produce for him. He was cursed, which was terrible, terrible. The Lord turned his face away from Cain, which was an awful punishment.

"But he did not kill him," McDade said, drunk in the warm June afternoon.

The saloon doors stood open onto the street. Old-timers sat at the bar or at marble-topped tables toward the back under gas jets that flared day and night and looked out at the yellow street, or up at the buzzing fly-twists, or down into their schooners. The barman was below, and they could hear barrels rumbling about under their feet. Now and then someone would walk by on the slat sidewalk outside, an aproned boy look in, a vegetable or fish man (Weber had been a huckster) shove his cart past crying out.

The point was he did not kill him. When Cain grumbled that people would know him and slay him because of the deed, God put the mark on him. People would see God's mark, His hand and seal, and not kill Cain. The purpose of the mark was to prevent capital execution.

"Whosoever slayeth Cain, vengeance shall be taken on him sevenfold."

"Is that the shorthand you're using? I'd like to do that. Any skill at all. A man ought to have a craft he can turn to in need, if he has to leave his position, say, and wants interim work. . . ."

"Yet here we go, don't we, against the first thing the book says on killing." Drunk, sly now, he could express this. "The punishment lay in what he did. He had killed his brother. His own brother lay dead at his feet, and God turned His face away. There was no necessity to kill Cain. The punishment was inside the crime, wasn't it? Yes, you may be sure it was. If Cain was killed, you had only another crime to handle, and it is in that point you find your great celestial wisdom, as I see it. Don't you punish the executioner? God knew when to stop.

"If I kill my brother I've killed myself. I'm dead anyhow. God, my neighbors turn their faces away. I don't find work whether I know shorthand or not, you see?—and I am cast out, a tramp: as good as dead.

"Didn't Mother Eve bear Seth to take Abel's place? So even that part was all right: a grieving mother comforted, you see? And didn't the good young Abel dwell forever in paradise on a throne? So what was missing? Each link of the chain was in place.

"The same with the son of God on his cross. 'Forgive them,' he said; and out of ill comes good at last."

He saw that the correspondent had closed his notebook.

More soberly McDade said, "I know how we must live in society—about the crime rate and all: the deterrent and protecting our kiddies. I'm no ostrich. But look at it now. . . ."

Weber was a man, not a dog, was what it came down to.

He had lost his audience. The reporter was asleep with his eyes open.

Well, wasn't it a fact that McDade himself did not believe in God? He had heard his own words going on here; he was a fraud, he thought, and sly: worse than a fraud, with his Bible-talk to score points with a young man.

Weber was a man, was what he knew for sure, sober or drunk.

And he, McDade, knew something about shorthand too, having observed the stenographers for years in the courts, which made him a bit more of a fraud. And he could no more do manual labor than sing an opera.

To the Cage This Prison, denying the appeal to the high court it seems they will kill you and I for 1 am delited, as aware of the wages. You killed not a man but a girl, you would not have fortutude to atak man with your ax, Jenny was her name in the paper. Since you need to kno I am in for grand larceny 2d degree, and dont kill a child who trusts me. A wif and 2 young ones outside await me, but who waits where you go??? The mulato my pardner up in the basket shop is a far better man than you, what we thro in the bucket stand, you kno, is better materiel for a man than you Weber. The Law and God are just to kill you, for if they let you go youll brain another por girl and leave her wallowing in her own blood. Use an ax to chop wood. Or youll brain some one in the asilum if they commute you. I was born in Nevada Territory where men are men and dont do that. Pardners we held our liqor and killed men in fair fight. Im 45 and alredy live 15 years more than you ever will. Now electricity will burn you slo the way the mohawks did in this state to a man not long ago and a good thing I say, remember the girl you killed when she was cooking your brekfast with the bloody ax, or better the barber who brings the kite may cut your throat and save the state a few frogskins. I must close running out of paper. Sin my name Jack Bell.

10 June '90

RUPERT WEBER, ESQ.
AT CLARKVILLE

. . . just the other Day good Chaplin Snow came to my cell at twilight. I looked and saw his pleasant Face at my grate. He stuck in a Finger which I shook and we had a Talk in part touching one Rupert Weber. The Chaplin is much Concerned with you. He said to me Weber is out of touch with GOD. He was Right with GOD and now he is not. Well I hope a word from a Con and fellow-sufferer may persuade you. The LORD is no off again on again thing. He is eternal, eternally Loving and Forgiving. Man alone is on again off again. If I could give you some of what I Feel, what I *know*, Weber, of the Real Living Presence of GOD in every man and thing on earth . . .

Well, poor Rev. Snow. He has his many Duties. As you know it is his first time on a Prison job. I have watched him age ten years in as many months. He has got his Religious Service both here and in the Insane Asylum adjoining which makes four and more (in Feast times) a week, then his Discussion Group. He reads Mail in and out (*not* this "Kite" rest assured). He must Visit in the Hospital every day the sick and dying and attend the poor "Kinks" as well, and searches out Friends and relatives of the Dead. There is the Library. Here is a sign of a regular fellow. He tells me on the side that he could just about do without the quality of Material sent into the Library by the W.C.T.U., so dull it "puts you to sleep." And "What a Boon is Work!" says Chaplin Snow worried over the evil of idleness in our Prison System, or he is there worried over some Con who is blue, or over his Evening School. Yet all is Nothing to his worry over R. Weber who in his Dark Night of Pain slipped away from his Shepherd. He wakes at midnight, finds one of the Flock strayed, and goes here and there calling!

(Lights Out)

With the dawn. I read this and think what a poor Thing it is! If my heart was a letter and you could read that you would be persuaded. GOD rescues us from Death if we trust in Him, just as our Free Spirit rescues us from every Prison of man.

M. O. WILSON, No. 46

DEAR WEBER

I saw the cut the artist did in the Clarkville rag and if your like that your handsome. I am another dutchman with you. A landlofer if you recall the words. Well its bad to kill you a sad waste. I am in for "Forgery and Attempts" two years 6 mos. but can think of plenty they could get me on would be your Molly any day. Get me? The word is you have less then 2 mos. to go. Will the electric scorch a shame to mutilate Weber. The word is you cant read who reads your kites to you? Am going to put some thing so small no one can read it but I will know I wrote it. . . .

DUTCHMAN (Rouse mit him)

15

"What do you say, Kernahan?"

The night watch rose and looked in at Weber from the door of his cubicle, the deep yellow light behind him so that he stood in the iron dark with radiance around him like one of the engravings of the saints. Weber, who had been pacing though it was three in the morning, now stood in one corner of his cage with his fingers hooked high in the mesh, hanging his weight from them, relaxed-looking. He said in his slow rusty voice, "That's all, ain't it? They'll do it now."

"Yes."

"When?"

"Buxton don't confide in me."

Weber said after a silence, slouching relaxed in the corner of his cage, "I'd like to know."

16

Buxton had been writing. Now he leaned back, pen suspended. He said from his reverie, "We had better go down and have a look at it," not moving.

His office was a pleasantly shadowed man's sort of place with leather-padded chairs and thick Turkey carpeting; there were brass spittoons and a slim bentwood cloak stand with the warden's umbrella hanging from one of its branches. Over the desk the electrolier with its orange-glassed lights was lit; on the desk were a pair of telephones and wicker correspondence trays.

Stone at the window said, "Yes"—also dreaming.

An unseasonable early mist lay on the farm garden. Guards and workmen were coming off for the evening, some to the prison entrance that was beneath where Stone stood watching, most to the adjoining asylum entrance. He observed a pair of heavy brown horses being unhitched from a harrow or horse rake—he knew nothing of such things—and led off, their thatched hoofs plodding. The plants stretched row on row for acres.

"We grow cabbages," said Buxton, answering an earlier polite question of Stone's, "and lettuce. Those are the principal items together with our celery." He managed to stir a little from his dream. "We earned nearly four hundred on those last year and ought to do as well this time."

Then he said, "I have settled upon the other man, Taggart, to take your place."

There were cows in a pasture beyond the garden—white specks wading in the flood of mist. Anxiety grew in the electrician as he looked out; unaccustomed to daydreams, he could not keep his mind on the subject. "Perhaps I should stay on," he said with an effort.

"If you want to come back, I would consider it. I need all the help I can get."

Buxton did not like Stone and liked Taggart less, though he knew neither well; he could not understand the minds of these technical men. He remained silent; each nodded now and then in the assenting way of dreamers, as if they were caught by the powerful evening and wanted to put off their task. Stone, who had rubbed his skimpy red hair into spikes, looked out at the light; that's right, he nodded, anxiety growing.

They had had a suicide at the asylum the month before, and Buxton was not finished with the reports. ". . . deplorable disintegration of prison industries and deterioration of *morale* of the prisoners as a mass, and an unprecedented . . ."

The inmate had been a model for years, getting well; and the warden had often passed the time of day with her: as quiet a little person as you could find, one not considered to have such tendencies. Dr. Clark had been upset. It drifted in and out of Buxton's mind now: the image of the woman alive who would drop a stiff old-fashioned curtsy when he passed; perfectly respectable, normal-appearing; he had proposed her to Mrs. Buxton as a candidate for the house to do the downstairs or a little sewing.

"Mrs. Buxton is unwell," he thought reluctantly.

Stone cleared his throat, turning.

17

The switchboard was fixed to the wall in what had been the death chamber before they moved the chair into the big room farther along. It was about three by five feet and contained, besides the panel with its two dozen lamps, the Cardew voltmeter Stone had repaired and reinstalled, the resistance box or Wheatstone bridge, rheostat, ammeter, and two switches—one to govern the lamp board, the other to complete the circuit through the death chair. The dynamo, which was housed in the far southwest corner of the prison, was connected to the switchboard by two heavy-gauge wires; one wire passed through the switchboard and led directly to the chair, the other passed through the ammeter and was intercepted by the execution switch. The voltmeter and resistance box were connected to each other and to the direct wire.

Buxton watched while Stone hunched over the board. The electrician wore a pair of rubber-lined gloves and a coffee-colored duster he had brought along in a bag.

When the circuit was completed through the resistance box, that measured a fixed amount of voltage; the voltmeter measured the remainder. A bell button on the board connected the board with the dynamo and engine rooms and was used to signal start dynamo, requests for increased pressure, and stop dynamo. When the dynamo developed high pressures, current snapped like branches breaking, and the switchboard room filled with an odor of burnt cloth and rubber.

They visited the lighting plant, which contained two lower-voltage dynamos in addition to the one Stone had bought for the State.

"Was it running at full speed?" Buxton asked the guard captain.

Two guards came up from the engine room beneath and stood awkwardly, their eyes on Stone and the warden.

"We did not receive above twelve hundred volts in pressure," said Buxton.

The captain laid a hand on the now stilled machine; a plate screwed to its red flank said: "Westinghouse Electric Co., Pittsburgh, Pa."

"That's ample," said Stone.

The captain could not say quite; he thought they could get a good deal more. "This old wood floor in here jumps like the devil when she goes, though, and the belt slips a bit."

"Vibration causes the slipping?"

"I believe so."

"That might account for a fluctuation we noticed on the voltmeter."

"You are comfortably within the range and miles above the minimum voltage required to get a couple of amperes of current through him," said Stone. Now that he was occupied the anxiety had left him.

18

They returned to the switchboard for another test, this time received 1,350 volts without detectable fluctuation, then inspected the chair itself, which was in the room adjoining.

It stood on a broad square of rubberized matting; the wall behind was half tiled in white; a large exposed electric lamp in a wavy collar of white glass hung over it and a bit to one side. It bore little resemblance to the reclining contraption like a heavy beach chair that Stone had originally designed and submitted. He had worked on it since; and others, notably a Rochester inventor and electrician, had developed it, working right here in a corner of the broom shop along with a pair of convict cabinetmakers. It was tall and straight now, had a high straight back only slightly tilted and a comfortable seat of flat padded leather; there was a cushioned rest for the head, which could be raised and lowered on an adjustable bar of wood. In addition to the forehead and chin straps there were nine straps and buckles designed to restrain the body and maintain firm contact with the electrodes. There were two electrodes, each ending in a cup-shaped rubber disc and sponge, the wires buried in the sponges, which would be soaked in salt solution. The upper electrode was held on a spring in a bracket screwed to the wood bar (the Rochester man had wanted to suspend coiled wire, electrode, and straps from the ceiling, but the sight of it had seemed ugly to Stone), the lower one ran up through a hole cut into the leather webbing at the rear of the chair's seat and was also kept in tension on a spring.

Stone tugged the straps, raised and lowered the head bar, and then, with energy, shoved the chair up against the tiled wall, rocking it as he did. He had made the strength of the chair an important point in building it and been critical of work that did not. At last he sat in it in his linen coat and nodded to Buxton who began buckling the straps. Stone's long pale face was crossed by straps that kept his head firmly against the cushioned back and covered his eyes; his forearms and wrists were strapped to the broad arm rests; there was a wide belt across his chest; the electrician's legs were confined separately at the ankles by belts a full quarter of an inch thick. He shook his blinded head to test Buxton's work. He tugged with all his might at the arm and leg straps, trying to rise. The last evening light streamed in from a high window opposite, turning the man's hair to flame. He was silent and pale. Buxton, the warden, moved in every action with firmness and decision, not speaking. Then he stood back and looked at Stone. Finally he undid the straps and released him.

four

The Trick

1

The only things outside of him were that clock of McDade's going and the roosters and other creatures on farms beyond the prison—their noise; and at dawn he had done no good, made no headway. And yes, there was the scrap of tree outside his window, its leaves swollen now, the sky through it a sort of yellow, and a star hanging in its branches.

He made sure anyway that the night watch did not sleep on the job. Kernahan was a bastard.

There was little thought for McDade. He supposed McDade was all right. Kernahan was a wrong one. Maybe your night force always was bad.

Cocks began their noise in every farmyard. Weber had all his clothes on because he was forever cold. Cold struck right down through him; his flesh was crawling cold, nose and ears like ice; night or day made no difference, though it was warm June.

He had few thoughts in words; they were mostly pictures. One was bringing fruits in the scales tray up to Jenny. That big girl in bed, her arms like silk, breasts sliding down over her chest, the spreading brown roses on them; and the bedroom morning smell that a man and woman always make together, so that her husband was there with them in a way, though he was gone on his job: that came back to him. But Weber was cold. They always said all the time that you get a hard arm out of being scragged, and now that was out, his first in how long? . . . his whole night's work, these couple of notions. The rest lay deep in a rubble of broken bits, a cityful of broken pieces, no two fitting together.

2

He was cold.

He had given the Bible and Common Prayer back to little Snow. His name, which Snow had taught him to write, was inside both books on the empty page, but he scored the autographs out before he handed them back; they were worth something, weren't they?

Hadn't Weber been down on his knees? The soft old man from in town, Baird: down on his old knees. The little cocky Snow: down like a runner with his blue eyes keen, looking through the walls it seemed, a red spot on each cheek. "Lead on, O King Eternal . . ."

"Dearly beloved, it hath pleased almighty God . . ." All right.

Each man was called a Protestant; one, Baird, called himself the Methodist, the other Episcopal; yet somehow both were both.

Didn't he confess everything?

Baird's old knees went off like pistols, but Snow came up like an athlete. Earlier Weber had been baptized in the name of . . .

". . . twenty-eight years old, was born near Millersburg, but came into Philly when I was young. After a flood it was. I at present reside in the rear of 367 South Pearl, Buffalo. . . . While

I was cleaning the horse Jenny come out to the barn and told the boy she wanted eggs. I went and fixed the stable door, then walked into the house with the hatchet in my hand that I fixed the door with. I first got acquainted with Jenny on Christian Street in Philadelphia when I was peddling. . . ." He had put an X at the end of the statement for his name. "Since I come to Buffalo I have been drinking considerable and had more or less quarrels with this woman Jenny. This morning, March 29th, '89, between 7 and 8 o'clock, I struck Jenny on the head with a hatchet—I don't know how many times—with the idea to kill her. . . ."

3

Snow described it. It was not the love in songs, and it was not the love with a hard arm that you did not talk about. It was something else.

The pictures came without his trying. LOVE and PITY were a woman waiting, no woman he had seen in life. She sat at a fountain in a white outfit that showed her divine form beneath, one bare foot visible peeping out. She leaned her white arm on the fountain wall and supported her head with it, looking into the water. But she was waiting for Weber. Weber would come there on the other side of DEATH, rising as if on wings, pulling a curtain aside; he would go to her with the love that was something else. He had never had a thought for the electricity, except that he understood it would work in an instant and not hurt him.

These were pictures like photographs against the back of his eyes: the other woman decked out in scarlet, carrying a cup full of abominations and the filth of her fornications. She had had written on her forehead "MYSTERY, BABYLON THE GREAT, MOTHER OF HARLOTS" and more. And Weber saw heaven.

Snow described New Heaven, and New Jerusalem, and After Judgment. (And would not Weber share? Chaplain Snow promised he would!) Well, it was all right, and the electricity was all right. Forget it.

Jewels had winked then when Weber shut his eyes, and he saw the spired, populous New Jerusalem rising to heaven's portals, pavilions, orchards, and golden viaducts sparkling—city raised on crystal city, pennants flung out, right on up to the green-watered meadows of eternal heaven itself where God's benign physiognomy, as Snow called it, burned like the sun. And *there* would be his woman at her cool fountain waiting, about to turn to him.

4

But then it dropped. There was nothing there. It had struck him dumb not to see it any more and to know there was nothing there. He did not have to wonder about it. It was gone. It was like the drink you had. The glass was empty, and you pissed, and that was it.

5

In his silence he rummaged fitfully for a time, picking up bits and discarding them. Then he was utterly quiet, deep as water. Everything had simply dropped away, Snow and Life Eternal were gone; the sun was out of the sky like a hot coal dropped into water. Snow came, but it was no good. And the woman, Buxton's wife with her book of sermons—she was no good: old but not old, her soft white face came at him like a moon in the dark.

He swam in fear. It was as if someone had picked him up and thrown him into a winter river or into that damned Lake Erie, and the water was Fear; it washed through him; he was drowning in it. Snow's fair small face swam there, and the old moon of a woman's. Kernahan yawning and stretching, the glasses at the end of his paw trembling; the barber who came and passed on kites to him . . .

He had fits of anger, spasms that shook him with rage. McDade would have read him the kites, but Weber threw them into the bucket at night. He took the bright chromo of John the Baptist and baby Jesus and the winter-white bird and, shaking with rage, used it though he knew he was empty, and dumped it into the bucket. If a dog barked at night in one of the city yards, he felt its life throwing off sparks in the darkness; the cocks at dawn were hot with life; but when they stopped, that was it, and they were dead; as much as was left of the dog or the cock after that was as much as Weber now knew of Life Eternal and New Jerusalem. The kites and John went into the bucket. Forget it. All the time he was drowning in fear.

It would not do. It was shit. It belonged with the kites and picture of Johnny in his odd shirt—up Weber's bum and into the bucket. But didn't he need something? If it would not do, what would? He could not think. The trouble was right there, in that—he couldn't think.

6

He forgot where he was. When the chaplain went to leave, Weber would go with him. Why not? Wasn't he tired of this and cold to the bone? Walk out; go home to Philly.

He could not think why he shouldn't.

"Not now, Weber."

Keough—he was a Molly, Weber could tell—tapping the loaded cane on the cage.

Wake up! Get up!

He could hear teams being worked in the prison farm, the trace chains singing, men shouting to each other across fields. He had been part raised on a farm. There were some sounds already inside your head before you heard them. If a crow called, he heard it beforehand, then again: he almost knew it would call. He knew if a horse was going to neigh; then it did; and when another would answer it, perhaps a mile off somewhere. He knew how all the old farm sounds went; how dogs started at night, one after another across woods and rivers, and couldn't stop; and the cocks with their blazing shouts at dawn: "Get up! Go to work!"

There was a lady in Indiana: *what?* She might as well be talking Latin: it would put the city fathers into a pickle. The word: *fathers*. People ("They were awful, Rupert!") singing "Annie Rooney"; he could hear that tune a bit in his head.

"You don't mean you don't want me?" he imagined she had said.

"P'r'aps not."

But though he did not want her she came: that pale old face swimming. No sun. She was dark and he was dark, crouched back in his cage like a stoat in a box. The woman's time was before. When he tried to picture her covered parts, it gave him a little cramp of disgust.

7

His friend Buffalo Billy—that's right—gave evidence: came in and saw it all, followed him out.

"What do you do for a living?"

"I huckster and I keep dogs."

"Fighting dogs?"

"No. One is a Newfoundland and the other is a conundrum. I don't know what he is."

He got a laugh on that. Billy was always full himself. The lawyer showed he was drunk in court too. They would both of them get full every day before supper and then fall down laughing; and Billy run his wagon like a madman when he was drunk. Good times: yes; yet they got through the day with almost everything sold but maybe a few cheeses, and he never once forgot to clean and put out his horse after. "Put him in the inebriate asylum," Billy would say, full himself, about Weber . . . years before, too, at Denny O'Brien's in Philly: yes. "We come away from her husband and my old bitch, took her little four-year-old girl, and come to Buffalo under the name Johnson as man and wife. . . . I washed myself and went out and cleaned my horses. Jenny come out and told the boy she wanted some eggs. I went and got the eggs and give them to her in a basket, then walked after her into the house with the hatchet in my hand I fixed the stable door with. . . ."

There was the child's rocker there. He took the little girl to the landlady. When he came back Jenny was flat out, there was a bloody handprint on the wall. "Then Billy come in."

"Why, I says to the bartender," said Billy giving evidence, " 'Do not give this man anything to drink. He has brained his wife, and she lays wallowing in her own blood.' And the bartender refused to serve him a drink. 'Yes, I have,' says Weber, 'and I am willing to take the rope for it, the sooner the better.' We left that saloon and headed for another. 'Ain't you going to get a doctor for her?' I says; and, 'Does the doctor live in a saloon?' 'No,' he says, 'just let me get a glass of beer here, and I will go for the doctor.' 'Is that a promise?' And then the police officer appeared and Weber went to him. The officer says to me, 'Will you enter a complaint?' 'Yes, I will,' I says. The officer asks him, 'Have you been licking your wife?' 'Yes,' he says. 'What did you hit her with?' He says, 'A hatchet.' I then asked him what he done it for there before the officer, and he told us that was to be found out."

It was no work to him to clean a horse, give it a brush; he enjoyed it. He had the one crock and one nice tall chestnut gelding with socks and a patch on its chest. He used the flat of his hands to beat the dust out of its hide, for they picked up lots of it in the Buffalo streets; then he pulled the stickers and junk out of its tail; then the currycomb with a lot of elbow grease behind it, all the time easing the horse with talk; the soft brush after that, and at last he would go over him with a piece of damped sacking to bring up the gloss, while the horse, liking this, stepped gently back and forth in the stall and bobbed its head. Weber did not mind taking out the stuff that built up in its hoofs and under the shoes, though it stank worse than you-know-what; nor did he mind working the red wax out of its sack.

Bucky. He guessed that horse was set up somewhere else now. He long ago signed the authority to his brother to sell his goods. That horse would be somewhere in front of a cart with other hands driving him. That was all right: forget it. Yet wasn't it odd that he would be dead and still Bucky going along in front of a wagon?

Then anger hit him a blow; he spat through the mesh of the cage, which brought McDade out. It would not do! Then fear; he thought, terrified, "No!"

8

He half liked getting out and onto the train, and half he did not like it. It made him dizzy after the quietness of his cage. But there were the farms to look at from the train, and the clean depots, and the courtroom big and airy as a Pennsylvania hayloft; they could talk Latin, he said, for all he understood of it. "A good deal of that they're saying *is* Latin, Weber," McDade replied. And Keough, the Molly, smirked.

It rained a little going back, and the new oats shone bright green. Puddles of water flew about the windowglass with the speed of the train instead of dropping straight down. When he moved his shoes he felt the train grit under their soles, Keough's hard little knees touching his.

"Well, your request for a hearing before the Supreme Court of the United States has been turned down, Rupert," said Buxton. "I am afraid you must be very disappointed."

He returned his King suit, and watch and chain, and wallet

and got back into prison issue. They waited in the warden's office until dark, then took him back to the cage.

"There will be company for you one of these weeks," the warden said.

Kernahan declared they meant to give the electrical execution two good tries at least.

His mother used to say, "You don't love me, or you wouldn't treat me so bad"—to him, his brother, his *father*. Love. Snow used the word the same way. All Weber had to do as a boy was come in from the street and there was the word hot in the house. She might as well say in another language what she meant: "EVERYONE THAT LOVETH IS BORN OF GOD" his mother stitched into the sampler. Snow used the same word like a woman, called it something else, though. It was all in a foreign language now. The warden's wife. "I don't want you." And she made a fiery knot of disgust in him, a little clenching of disgust in his manhood.

Love.

One morning, after the application had been denied, he woke unable to breathe. He was choking for breath. He gasped horribly, wide awake, dying—it would save the State something—until he saw Kernahan staring fiercely, angrily in at him, weighing the billy in his hand. Then he was all right.

His father had been on a provision and forage train, a Federal soldier and one of Grant's heroes: 3rd Division, II Army Corps. He had been wounded at Chancellorsville and had a paper signed by U. S. Grant. Too bad he had not died.

For his mother's memory Weber let Snow sell him the bill of goods. "Lead on, O King Eternal" . . . "Stand up for Jesus."

> Abide with me! Fast falls the eventide;
> The darkness deepens; Lord, with me abide! . . .

But it was dry after all. That sack was an empty one. He was too late. It was all shit and into the bucket with it.

Now there was the dynamo—so he believed it was called; he

did not know the first thing about it. Though it was located in another corner of the prison, he could hear its hum. Two others worked the shop machinery, but this big one made its own sound, and when it was going and they ran a test he could hear the crackling like a fire of green sticks and smell the scorch. Then when they did a living thing, like their calf, he could smell its fresh babyish dung and burnt hair. It did not bother him.

A skinny glass of water with red hair and a scared face: the electrician glanced in at Weber fast, then turned as if someone had called.

Snow did not come after the appeal was denied, and Mrs. Buxton did not come for a week. Bush the lawyer came, though, and the warden, and another, new electrician. Dr. Clark came and checked him over, made him take off most of his clothes so that he shivered on his bunk like a starved dog, tapped him, and listened to him. He asked him why he did not bathe.

"I could not bear the smell of myself if I were you."

"I couldn't bear the smell of you neither," Weber joked.

Weber spoke nothing, sulking, when Snow came at length. The chaplain apologized. "I had to go to Elmira to see my mother who is ill, Rupert."

He was looking at the convict with closeness: a particular thing was to be said. "We are afraid that she is perilously ill, in fact. My sister Virginia is living with her now, and I've brought my little nephew, her boy, home with me." He sat on the edge of the prisoner's bunk, and as Weber paced the young minister's glance followed him. "Rupert, we are certain she is dying"—hurling the hard word straight out, cheeks blazing.

Nothing from Weber, but the sulky look had gone; he paused in his pacing and turned to McDade as if he were going to ask him to let the chaplain out. But he said nothing. He guessed Snow was selling a bill of goods.

"She knows she is dying, Rupert."

There. He was not the only one, that meant.

"Brother, it isn't as if we expected your application to be accepted."

And then: "Shall I leave?"

Weber said at last, "So your mother is sick."

"I am afraid so."

"I guess she's old."

She was fifty-five.

She was old, and everyone's days, marked out in white or black, came along. It did not matter. They were split up—good, bad; you were ahead or you were behind; you had more of the one thing or more of the other, depending on the luck you happened to be born with. Weber could tell that, though Snow thought it was, this was not unlucky.

"It ain't so bad."

Snow did not understand.

"Death," Weber said awkwardly. He did not speak of dying but of the sweetness of death.

He started to say more, then did not. The chaplain was not interested in his own bill of goods, though he pretended to be; he was only afraid for his mother.

"Why do *you* think it's not bad?"

"Well, I know it."

It seemed to puzzle the chaplain, as if he wanted to be pleased but could not be.

In the morning, finally, Mrs. Buxton came. The sun flared behind her pale head. She stood outside of his cage just at the spot where the sun came down, as if she were deliberately hiding in it; her features were hidden.

He said, answering her question, "I'm all right."

The room seemed smaller with her in it. McDade, tilting back in his chair, heavy in his dark serge, seemed closer, larger, the golden N.Y.S.P. on his cap brighter.

"I apologize for not coming. Mr. Buxton says it is the heat that affects me, and he has restricted my prison visits to one day a week. I go to the hospital and asylum, and then to a few of my special favorites, including you, and then I am about used up. I think you've all enjoyed your holiday from me and my chatter, though you're too polite to say so." She said, "I can imagine what it has been like for you, Rupert—this terrible news."

Weber felt perfectly fine: "It's all right."

"I wish they had not taken you on the train. I know that for myself a taste of freedom would be worse than prison."

Unaccountably, Weber felt fine. It was a fine sunny morning.

He had had his breakfast with an egg; he felt still the heat of the good bootleg in him; the warm sun was on his bunk lighting each hair of the blanket so that it trembled and shone like a bishop's cloak; and there where he put his weight on it was his outspread hand planted in the center of the bunk on the flaming blanket, yellow-brown in that abiding sun. McDade sat on his chair beyond the woman, tilted back, legs straddled, glowing; he was like a prince. Unaccountably, Weber felt fine. He had never felt better in his life. Nothing in the world was wrong, and he had never felt better.

9

He remembered that storm on the farm, the freshet coming down. It started one April day with a light wind and then the clouds building, sliding across each other, so that their substance grew more and more dense; the sun disappeared, and it was as black as night. First a little rain sparkling like hot grease. And then, in the middle of April, hailstones pounding down, their gunfire everywhere: on the roofs of the sheds and barn, clattering on the implements. His father watched from the window, and his brother, and so did he. Smells of earth rose powerfully; and that thick farm smell of grease and paint, cattle dung and straw, the blood smell of iron—as powerful as a living breath. He felt his hands on the sill as he looked out. Their farm was in a hollow, and everything poured right into it and then backed up on them again from the ridges around after the earth and trees had drunk their fill. A river came down on them, a cataract. His father and brother, too late, went out to the cattle and got a few back; they were all half swimming; they got three into the house, right in the kitchen there. They stood in swirling water in the house. His mother shrieked and hollered. What sort of a fool would build down in that hollow anyhow? The horses drowned; the chickens; most of the cows. When it drained off they all went out, going into mud to their knees. Their dog Bonny lay dead, starting to bloat. The hogs—the good lard hogs—were drowned, the sow's new litter too. Cats floated in little lakes in the muck of the barnyard; rats and mice were everywhere drowned; cattle lay choked in their stalls; the horses with their heads up and stiff, coats matted wet and muddy, trying to get out still as they died; later they were just like scraps of old dried leather, curled in death: death on every hand. Their little two-room house, though it stood on a rise in the midst of the hollow, had had water in up to two and a half feet; the rugs and bedding and much of the furniture were ruined. The floors his father had cut with his own hand were ruined and sprang up, twisting like snakes when they dried; their staples were ruined; the house cats were drowned. For weeks afterward they found dead things, domestic and wild, wherever they stepped, and the stink of it all, along with the failure of it, the inability to prevail over it, drove them out at last with what they had remaining filling less than half of the compost cart, his father pulling, his brother pushing, him and his mother inside.

He thought of this now and felt all right. It did not trouble him that the memory was not a bad one. They had gone through the town on their way east to Philadelphia and seen the damage there, and that had been all right too: the streets washed out, muck two feet thick on the courthouse lawn, furniture and bedding still out of doors drying, the sweet dead stink of death everywhere. It was painful to everyone but him, and it had been a comfort to him. It made him swoon with pleasant sleepiness then as it did now. His God was sweet death swelling everywhere.

Well, the man's mother was dying.

It was like the baptism all over again during that long afternoon. He had never felt better.

But then by dusk it dropped away again—the little courage and comfort; the sun was out of the sky in more ways than one; he struggled in fear again, drowning. "No!" It would not do! And when Snow came on his vesper call he spoke at last.

10

"I don't know what you mean," Snow replied. "What is it?"

Weber shook his head and glanced over at Kernahan, who was just on duty, as if humorously to include him in a plain man's helplessness.

"What it is I'll tell you," Weber said at length, sounding "dutchie"—"I can't think."

"I see that you must think about what's coming."

"P'r'aps. Well, yes!"

"I will help you."

Weber sat bundled in all his clothes, shivering violently, and Snow, after observing him, said in alarm, "Why don't I ask Corporal Kernahan to go for the night physician, Rupert?"

"I don't want a doctor."

Another wait.

Snow lowered his head, laced his fingers, and the convict saw he was praying. Looking at him do it, seeing that yellow hair and clean pink scalp, gave him the odd cramp of disgust. "Don't do that," he said urgently. "It's no good to me.

"I'm right out of it, don't you see? Your way don't help. I can't think what's right."

"Let me help you." And then: "Brother, what do you mean? You talk about a trick."

"Well, I mean to go like a man. That's the trick."

It was said. It wasn't death but that he could not be afraid of dying and do the trick. He looked at the other narrowly. Snow nodded. He said, "It indicates a line to take. I must try your viewpoint. I do see."

Weber paced in a rage. The little cock gave him nothing back. Hadn't he gone to work and said it to him? He had given him something at last and knew nothing would be returned. He raged, pacing most of the night. He picked up the lid of the bucket and spat into it. There went the little man—the parson: into the bucket with everything! What was in that kite? Snow is the shepherd, Weber the sheep who has strayed, and Snow goes here and there calling. That was a yarn. He had stopped McDade reading, taken the kite, and thrown it into the slops. Where does Weber stray locked up? He supposed he knew who had strayed.

He made certain Kernahan did not sleep. "What do you say?"—prodding him. He wanted to know the date, the hour; the night watch had to be lying when he said he did not know.

"Buxton don't take me into his confidence," said the keeper again. "But be sure I won't neglect to tell you when he does."

five

At Dead Center

1

The silence that precedes a warden's or keeper's rounds was tonight exasperating out of proportion. Buxton climbed the hot galleries. The slop jars waiting outside cells, flies swarming on their lids, the permanent mixed smell of tainted meat, damp, and disinfectants that was as much part of the prison as its walls, the sliding foxy looks of the cons, the guards' muffled make-work air in his path: all was offensive. He was highly irritated. After lights-out sighs and groans of prisoners—sounds he had known for years—irritated and troubled him. The safety in the drugstore, like a corpse under the white gas jet, saluted. Buxton, mouth and nose covered with a handkerchief, glanced into the ward beyond. The brass-knobbed beds creaked with the restless, sweating sick. Keough was told to note that the water cooler was empty; also surgical cabinet unlocked, door ajar, a syringe unnoticed in the dust on the floor beneath it, canes and crutches hooked over the bed rails—all contrary to regulations. Buxton grew uneasily ill-tempered: a measles in quarantine, a possible consumption. A man was rattling behind curtains at the end of the ward, and Buxton who knew he ought to go to him did not: Breen, white, Irish, seventy years old, State Labor, intemperate habits, three years for assault. Two others had died in the past few days, a first degree manslaughter, a first degree larceny. Keough tapped his loaded cane up and down the galleries from block to block. Screws were punishing one down in the jails—not disguising it; the warden heard his cries. "I think he is a bug, Warden," said Keough. "He don't stop shouting all night, which keeps the others awake. And he has diarrhea. That troubles them too."

"The man should be in hospital, not in the jails."

"He ain't that bad."

No doubt Keough was right.

He chose the week beginning Monday, August 4th, to kill Weber and, though the new law required him to be, was not more specific than that in his communication. Mr. Rose, the Governor's secretary, wrote back privately to say that Hill was displeased by this use of the warden's power to contravene a warrant's indication. But Buxton was indifferent. The warrant had not yet reached him. He told a reporter that he would see the job done well, that he was best judge of when it ought to take place since his hand was the one that would turn the lever at last. In any case, he would signal the moment.

In his mind he fixed on Wednesday, August 6th, in the morning, and after a day's further thought informed Chaplain Snow, and left it to Snow to tell Weber.

six

Snow in July

1

Snow would bend his head, put his slight hand across his eyes.

"Eternal God, father of us all"—seeing each word he spoke: "thou to whom I turn every hour for help, please to help me turn also this man Weber. He has known little love in his lifetime. . . ." If Weber on his bunk stirred, showed his impatience, Snow would stop. He would stop now even silent prayer if Weber stirred.

He was waiting.

You did not carry a long face into the condemned cage, so he was cheerful. Everything was toward a new beginning, like a new Creation: as if nothing had gone before. Between them—and this would be exalting—they were going to manage that "trick." Wasn't that it? Never mind that Weber gave few replies. Snow had the energy, had it to spare.

They were beginning again.

"Well, shall it be monologue today or dialogue?"

Leave things pending; as ready as a good servant: "I feel you are not bitter today, brother."

Weber would say, "I ain't"—his voice indifferent.

He need not use the opening. He could talk about the weather instead.

He would talk about the weather, what was going on in the prison or town, about himself. He was oblique, a schemer now; no, he did not stick at that: submit to a new Creation, find how he could serve. Men said to other men, provoked—he had heard it on the construction jobs, out in the yard, foremen and screws to the men: "Use your head, won't you?—your top floor." Snow could use his top floor.

". . . father of us all . . ."

Then break off and wait.

These were two men in colloquy. Weber had to think? He had his trick to do? They would manage.

Exaltation to one side, Snow saw that he might astonish himself before anyone else. Weapons in plenty lay everywhere rusting for a precedent. He would pick them up at random.

"*I* am afraid too." He could not sermonize upon it. Snow would never strut before death; indeed, it was pride to do so. But he supposed humility had its poor side; he knew he would be sadly bowed, useless before death, without help. He talked to Weber about his mother who was ill. He told him about the other recent personal terror: the return of that childhood phenomenon; and, surprisingly, this developed a cruel little bond between them.

"What do you mean I get small?"

"It is retinal . . . an ailment, I suppose, of vision. It is as if you are being carried down a long corridor or tunnel away from me. Light comes through from the open end of what appears to be a tunnel, and you grow smaller until you are the size of my hand. It terrifies me. It's a sense of having lost you, I think; the figurative losing sight of you is behind it."

"I don't get little."

Snow described it patiently. It was an occurrence of a physical nature entirely, he said finally, retreating. Weber stared.

The convict told Snow he did not like it—how he got smaller in the other's eyes; he did not want that happening. It became an engagement between them. Snow felt no need to be doctrinaire. Anything did for a start. One day Weber said he had dreamed about it. He was getting smaller, and he had awakened rolling on the cell floor, so that Kernahan came in uncertainly, ready with the weighted billy.

It made a nettlesome bond between them.

2

Snow's life was ecstasy to him. However, wryly, he modified the word, or however briefly the particular moment stayed to dazzle him, it was ecstasy—joy and light. Every thing (*two* words) of God, whether or not visible (whether or not mentionable: that's right), would create an ecstasy or, same thing, terror in him; all was light and love looming suddenly up and as suddenly darting off, plummeting down. Why had he assumed that Weber's gray emptiness was to be valued? It was worth nothing; light only had value, not darkness. Father, wasn't it true that formerly he had hidden joy from Weber thinking it would hurt a man who had soon to die?

Well, that was an error.

Bring light, show your light! Look out! What *was* the point in your minister of God bringing gloom, darkness, restraint, *sympathy* to a man in darkness? Mere sympathy when identity was asked: identity, if he could do it, saying simply, "I am also afraid of the pain of death." But *sympathy* was carrying darkness to one in the dark: let in the hot light of Joy!

He astonished himself.

What was it the poet said? No explorer before the discovered shore was more astonished and thrilled, no Spaniard upon his peak in Darien . . . "round many western islands" had he been. Now this was something else.

It alarmed his wife when he tried to tell her this. They strolled along the lake embankment. The three girls and his sister Virginia's boy were ahead of them, the boy going at his own pace, aloof. Cars and hacks and buggies, the few good carriages washed for Sunday, rushed up and down. Sun flashed in Snow's eyes, so that he had almost to close them. He would say no more to her. She was herself light. But it gave him a pang that she could not enter this world of Weber's with him, because he knew how it terrified her, how she made it worse than it was.

"But I took it for granted that you told him the truth."

"Only the safest fraction of it. Now I tell him all the truth, so far as I perceive it—about myself, unremote—and it is clearer to me now—what I must do concerning this trick of his."

It alarmed her.

"Is he frightened?" she asked, pale. She could not bear the thought of Weber's fear. She called out, "Belle, take Rosie's hand!" The boy, Carpenter, slouched miserably because he missed his mother. Snow lifted his hat. Reverend Baird, who was a widower, his daughter in the carriage with him: Baird lifted his hat and gave his wicked grin; if he was on his way to pastoral work at the Home in the park, that did not mean there was no sun in the sky. "A handsome family, Mr. Snow!" he shouted. Cyclists dashed up and down on the macadamized side paths and on the roadway, weaving among the horses.

He saw Kernahan cycling with a strange man—probably a reporter. They rode knee to knee, the keeper in a checkered cap.

Snow said to her, "He is not frightened in the sense I think you mean." He did not believe the condemned man rehearsed in constant terror the method and certainty of his death, remembering, sick at dawn, returning every moment to how it would be, sicker, more appalled each time.

They sat outside at home. The lilacs were finished, but large papery poppies stood in the cutting beds; there were iris and foxglove. Invading their lawn from adjoining pastures came the sky-blue chicory that his mother called frugality's flower; pungent mustard still bloomed hotly along the fences. (MOTHER IS RATHER BETTER AND SENDS HER LOVE. I LONG FOR CARPENTER. OUR LETTER FOLLOWS . . . ran the telegram in his pocket.) The miserable boy, and Rosie, little Annie, and his shy Belle were like stars in the dark grass; their voices went straight up like smoke. Dazzled, heavy-lidded, Snow let the gift of the day flash against his eyes. Weren't the children and his wife, the flowers and the telegram benefactions? Wasn't it all—including Weber's darkness and fear— a benefaction unprecedented in his experience?

3

"Why is she poor?" asked Weber.
"She is so shy"—speaking of Belle. "It's in me. I am the same."
Weber shook his head irritably.
That would serve.
"And your mother won't die?"
She was no longer perilously ill.
Weber sat puffed in his layers of clothing like a pigeon; he had that bird's affronted look; his hands trembled.
"Rupert, I suspected her illness could give you comfort."
Silence.
Snow, excited, saw that he had offended the man.
"I suppose I wanted you to know the worst to give you comfort."
"You could wish that on your mother?"
The man gave him a hard look.
Another day, "You are an odd one," Weber said.
That would do.
He told the convict something else:

"When you spoke after your silence and said, 'It would not go'—you remember? I came and we sat as we are now, and I asked what you meant by it. Well, brother, I *knew* you would point to the book on your table." This distressed him particularly, and talking of it now both distressed and excited him. He supposed he had not realized until this moment what it meant. "You said something along this line: 'That's what won't go—that in there, in that book.' I knew before ever you said it that that was what you meant."

Weber did not understand.

"Why, I suppose it means I hadn't enough faith in the things I taught you—in *any* case in the efficacy of my instruction and prayer." Snow's voice shook; he said with a laugh, "Now I am surely frightened." But it was all right. It was a more dangerous game—call it a game—than any he had thought to play. The bonds it forged were galling, as the leg irons must gall the convicts. But it was right. And the slippery silences in the cage—part of the game, too—were right.

Buxton set the date: August 6th in the morning. The chaplain went straight down and told him.

"All right."

"We have time to teach ourselves something."

He could not report these conversations to Mrs. Snow. They were in a sense terrible. Baird would not approve, nor any churchman of his acquaintance: this was no usual style of pastoral duty. But he knew he was not wrong. There was something between them now: these nettles they passed back and forth: Death, Fear. Weren't the two of them human? It was no matter of comforts, empty or not: "We will soon follow you"—no! They were talking about one man's certain, imminent death by untried means, talking about that trick. And *wasn't* it astonishing after all—the light of truth? Look at it! It could shine in the darkness even of this place! It would! Dazzling! Less of Saint John, if you don't mind, more, much more, of one man's hand reaching out in the dark to touch another's.

Not long after this Weber said, "I guess I am just as odd as anyone else."

Which meant, "Yes, I wished her dead."

And talking of light . . .

His family sat in the garden at dusk on July 4th to watch the town rocket display. A prison trusty, gardener by trade and convicted burglar who had been assigned recently to his house, leaned on his rake behind their chairs and watched too. Snow observed the good-looking tableau from his windows. Someone's hand moved in the half dark, and as if it were a signal the rockets began scoring angrily up the sky to bloom and ignite the faces, wholly revealed then—the convict's dull face beloved and revealed as well.

He asked Weber what he had thought of it.

"I couldn't see nothing."

"We could see the display from here, but Weber wouldn't look," McDade said. All right. Snow felt at ease. He no longer hid his pleasure if he felt it.

4

Well.

"The fact is that with God there is that clear intent to get good out of evil, don't you know? Our Lord's crucifixion is the first example, I mean to say first in importance. Out of that greatest evil, indeed, came our greatest good. . . ." It was not going. He talked about Joseph and his brothers: hadn't his brothers done Joseph a great evil, and hadn't great good come of it? "Rupert . . . ?"

God's intent was that out of Weber's suffering would come a new and humane technique for the lawful taking of human life.

Reiterate that.

If it did not quite "go," Snow was aware of a flicker of interest. The man was dark, curled in upon himself suspiciously, like a dark captive animal; only Snow could have detected the slight interest.

"With your help we are developing—will have developed and proved—this swift painless method for needful execution."

There was something: a little flutter of interest like a dog's before it lifts its head.

Yet even with such a "steer" he hesitated.

He spoke to Clark and asked the advice of those few of his regulars who really knew something about it. Snow sat casually on the platform, fair and supple as a boy; the men lounged in the front benches of the chapel, stained by color from the windows. They were fond of Snow and these times of consultation and spun them out circumlocutionally; this was their club. But when it came to it they said simply enough, as Clark had, that he ought to go ahead. Rather self-consciously a forger, the best educated of the lot, said, "Let there be light."

Exactly.

He stood looking out at that strange new land that was the world's future. It was full of threats, heavy as blood with tragedy. But looked at clearly it would contain as well these astounding gifts. How could Snow, of all people, be ungrateful and turn away from the offered bequests of God? And, honestly, hadn't he lost sight in the early months of the fact that the purpose of the new law—setting aside the matter of the warring electric power interests—was identical with God's purpose?

He raised the subject then.

"I was onto that myself," said Weber surprisingly.

5

"I started to think about it. That lawyer was here again." He meant Bush. He was, for Weber, talkative. "He worked over the machine with Buxton and that new executioner of theirs, then come in here and sat down. He said they was all over that machine with a fine-tooth comb."

Snow was meant to understand something.

"He says he don't like it." And then: " 'You must know,' he says, 'that we have based all our case upon the machine's uncertainty.' 'Why, yes,' I says, 'but it ain't uncertain. It's certain.' "

"So it is." Was that all?

Weber turned his hungry parrot profile to him, dropped the lid over one bright blue eye. Snow could not tell what he was meant to understand.

"Why, the lawyer says it's uncertain, and he ain't the only one to say it. Now I believe Bush wants me to act out I'm crazy." He had with him a kite that Kernahan had brought in the night before. It was, apparently, from a prisoner, unsigned, and in a fair, schooled hand:

Weber, your dynamo cannot generate in excess of 1150 volts sure, and that is not enough pressure for the purpose of the machine. You have the right to inquire into this and make a complaint, Weber, the right to be certain. The pressure must be at least 1500. To be sure, it should be 2000, do you understand? Moreover, the pressure must be *steady*. If it wabbles, going up and down, which there is reason to believe this dynamo may do, it will not properly perform its job.

It put Snow off. He wanted time to think.

He only said, almost automatically, "It's nonsense, Rupert. The dynamo is in perfect operating order."

McDade told him aside that several times when he came on he found Weber in a sort of fit, choking for breath. Kernahan said it was all right; the night man just raised his voice at him and he came around. "I thought you'd want to say a word to Dr. Clark on it."

First he spoke to Buxton in the warden's office. "What is Mr. Bush up to? He has upset my man. I am angry about it."

"I think he hopes to gather enough evidence of instability to warrant a stay and a Lunacy Commission investigation. A lawyer will always have a shot, you know, Hannibal. It isn't unreasonable."

"He deliberately frightened Rupert and invited him to take part in a collusion."

"I don't think so. Did Weber say Bush actually asked him to act crazy?"

"It was his impression. He is not crazy. Another stay will be insufferable." Snow's cheeks were scarlet. He kept edging around the warden's desk to look at his face, but the other gazed out of the window.

"Clark is keeping a record, as a matter of fact, a history of Weber's mental deterioration."

Snow said hotly, "I observe no deterioration."

"All right, Mr. Snow."

The subject was closed.

Snow then told him about the kite that had gotten into the prisoner's hands. It was not the point, perhaps, but Kernahan had no business delivering notes of any sort—nor had McDade; everything was supposed to cross the chaplain's desk, to which Buxton agreed. But the contents of the kite did not alarm the warden. "The dynamo is capable of generating enough pressure to kill him faster than the speed of light. Our new electrician has assured me of this, as did Stone recently. There will be no sensation whatsoever."

He answered a further question, his tone increasingly formal: "If there is a felon in this prison who is a trained electrical expert, I am unaware of the fact, and all former occupations are listed, as you know. Furthermore, the information this man has picked up is inaccurate. I have been into the subject thoroughly, as you may imagine, because I am sensitive to my heavy responsibility in it. I am assured that even a pressure of a thousand volts will do the job with perfect efficacy. You may like to tell Weber that if it is now an open subject between you."

The warden inquired into the condemned man's spiritual state, as if to say, "Here is your work." He was stiff and formal.

"I am uncertain about him. It's difficult."

When he tried to say something of what he wanted to do with Weber it sounded odd even in his own ears; and the warden, after a pause, said pointedly, "Well, I won't tell you your business, Mr. Snow. I am sure he will be as well prepared as possible, taking into account his natural mentality." And then: "There will be no further delay notwithstanding Bush's efforts."

"I am sorry for you"—seeing the man's exhausted look as he turned at last, the darkened eyes, Snow said, ". . . having to do this."

"I allow that Mrs. Buxton is upset. We have never had one that has not been commuted. This one will not be. The influence in favor of testing the new law is impressive and on very high levels." He added heavily: "We're getting a new man whom we must kill, by the way—from Sing Sing; our machinery is in operation and theirs is not nearly ready. I'll give you plenty of notice of his arrival. You and I are going to have our work cut out for us. . . .

"About the same. Stephen Clark sees her, and Dr. Widtman comes in from Syracuse twice a week. She must remain in bed for the present. Widtman says the trouble is, in part, all of this" —and he made a gesture that included the dark office with its winking brass and electric lights, the prison, Weber, Clarkville itself.

Snow made his hospital rounds. A man had died in the night, and now here was his little yellow pine coffin no bigger than a child's on a couple of trestles outside the infirmary, the safeties, specialists from the carpentry shop, with it; they gave Snow shy sliding smiles, and he had a word with them. When he saw Clark he asked his question at once.

"We are bound to find deterioration, physical and mental, after the year Weber has put in," Clark replied.

"I never thought you were serious the day you spoke of symptoms at my house."

"I was not particularly."

They walked out together, crossing the central yard with its gas lamps shining in the trees, and going around through the east court where, as almost always, coal cars were being unloaded. Customarily, administration took a leisurely pace before prisoners. "How they love the hardest physical labor!" said Snow with a kind of passion, watching a man who had cut off his jacket sleeves to be cool. "And it's the grandest thing in the world for them. There is our problem with the jails and the condemned cells—lack of useful activity."

And then: "Are you keeping a record of Weber's condition for Mr. Bush?"

"No."

But after they had talked for a moment to the guards on the main gate, been let out, and gone some way down Empire Street, Clark said, "I am keeping a record for the State, which employs me to do so." And when Snow began a sort of apology: "Nonsense. What else? You're not finished with me yet. . . .

"I've heard about the fits of choking. McDade's a nervous Nellie. There's nothing in it."

"They are not a symptom for your report?"

"No, they are not. He has a common spring catarrh and must work it off after hours of lying flat. I agree that the solitary prisoners are on their fundaments too much."

Snow slept badly that night thinking of Weber, defining again and again his duty to him; but even in the rawest, most difficult hours of the night ecstasy could lift him. He would deal with his terror for Weber's soul.

He had no fear of any function of himself, soul, mind, or body, and he believed he had no fear of others' functions. He recalled the carpenters' looks across the coffin, the sly cat's fondness from them; he had sensed their wish to touch him, because of him and because he held just the right keys for them—to rub up against him like cats. His manhood was not mysterious to him or fearful; it was one with his breath; nothing that he contained or that proceeded from him was other than perfectly, fractionally just— proper, decent, proportional (he thought this at three in the morning); nothing in his body or in the bodies of others was otherwise than lovely. Then how could death, which was the most violently effectual function of the body, delivering as it did that gorgeous fast-caged phoenix to the Lord, be other than lovely; nay, how could the instrument, the cause—disease, accident, age, and even this new humane electricity for the justly condemned—not be praised? He was exalted by his rendered understanding. In the dawn he padded about wearing slippers and robe, steering through the smoky darkness of his house, turning over books whose titles he could not see, scattering the pages of notes on his desk. He gazed exalted through a parlor window, saw the old elms that had been planted before the Revolution flat against the sky, and the headlong horses of cloud skidding behind them. He looked over the embracing earth and trees eastward across water—he vowed he saw it—and across old England, and endless cold steppes and peaks, across the sleeping and waking, dead and living; he observed, he was sure, the numberless dead eased in dark paradise. Well. Never mind. . . . Exhausted, he saw that brief vision like the objects lightning shows in a dark room, and no more.

Now, in a nervous way, he visited his sleeping children and young nephew in their bedrooms, padding agitatedly up and down stairs; he was . . . electrified. Exactly! His thoughts flew skyward unfinished: shreds of flame up a chimney; and at last he flung himself onto the sofa in the parlor and thought, "*No.*" And, desperately, feeling as if the life were being wrenched from him: "It won't go! It won't do"—using Weber's words. It would not do. He had forgotten himself and his duty entirely—all was wrongly defined. It would not go down! It was as if the life had been pulled out of him, and he fainted into sleep.

"At that point I dozed," he recalled, "worn out by these visions and thoughts and I suppose unable to bear that sense of disappointment. . . ."

His dream:

Reverend Baird was strolling one afternoon. He wore cream flannels, a bright old leghorn hat, and though it was warm his jacket and shirt with lay collar, and a rather striking tie. He also had on a pair of kid gloves. He stood by the lake and looked out at it appraisingly, shading his eyes against a great wheel of sun that filled the sky above him.

He said to Baird, "But when I woke up on the sofa with the sun on me it was all right. It had come clear in my mind while I slept. Don't you know I dreamed of you? You said, 'You shall fade suddenly like the grass, which in the morning is green and groweth' . . . praying as you had in Weber's cage in April, yet in an unfamiliar tone: '*Go ye accursed* into the fire everlasting, prepared for the devil and his angels.' It was unlike you. Then I saw you were addressing me, not Weber: 'No peace,' you cried in my ear, 'for the wicked!' It was unlike you."

But this preceding dialogue had been also in his dream.

Snow saw his wife.

"Are you all right?"

He felt ill and empty. Was he all right? Bother!

Sitting on the sofa in rational sunlight, he described Reverend Baird's costume in his dream; it made her smile.

6

FOR WEBER'S SAKE
Good friends, I'm weary of the way,
Of trumpets loud in wasteful war,
Of hypocrites who say they pray,
Of "education's" feckless lore,
Of waiting, waiting on this shore.
Frail men, frail women, all farewell,
Sweet children at your play;
Oh, hark you well the tolling bell
And list you as I pray—
Poor captives, here's the last resort;
Come, sue for your release.
Petition now our Highest Court
To lie in the Lamb's warm fleece.
God knows in Death alone is peace!

7

"The barber brought that," said McDade.

"Do you understand it, Rupert?" There were several poets among the convicts, Snow knew. Though it was anonymous, he thought he could tell who had written this. He had picked it out of a number of kites on Weber's table, read it, and then read it aloud.

"It's grand," said McDade from outside the cage. Weber said nothing. He was fingering his chin.

"It is sad and hopeless. I wish it were not so hopeless. But I imagine it appeals to your Celtic soul, Sergeant McDade." The keeper did not smile.

"You can just put those in the bucket," Weber said. "The poem too."

"I don't think . . ."

"I'll dispose of them," said McDade mildly. "The chaplain isn't your servant."

"That bastard Stern . . ."

"I wish you wouldn't destroy anything so well done as that poem," Snow said, tired.

"Stern gave me the hell of a cut shaving." The convict fingered the nick on his chin. He sat turned away from the others, sulking. "The bastard."

McDade said, "Mind."

"But *I* don't mind," said Snow. "Can't you leave us for a few minutes, Sergeant?"

McDade went back into his cubicle. Snow could see his plump knee, a hand upturned and the end of the billy dropping regularly into it. The guard was offended.

"I suppose you don't understand the poem, and that's why you don't like it."

Weber shrugged; he said, "It might as well be in Latin. What petition?"

"He's speaking of the beauty of death."

A shrug. He said after a moment, not lowering his voice, "Stern said the cons say I should have a try for insanity."

"Will you?"

"I guess I am loony or I ain't. The doctor would know."

"You are not."

"Well." He gave his dry gasp of laughter. "I mean p'r'aps I am."

It was the sort of dialogue Snow discouraged at any time.

"As you say, Dr. Clark would know."

Keough came down to inspect the condemned cages and give Weber his tobacco ration. "You haven't washed," he said to the prisoner.

"All right, Molly."

That was nothing to the principal keeper. He passed the tobacco over in his covert way and, while Weber rolled his first cigarette, went through the bedding and looked under the bits of furniture; he also went through the clothes Weber wore, patting him smoothly here and there while the convict smiled sardonically. Keough inspected the keepers' quarters as well, and looked in at the switchboard and at the chair in the room beyond. Finally he asked McDade in a loud voice, "Don't he bathe, Keeper?"

"He won't."

"It's all those clothes he has on. He'll poison himself to death before ever we get a chance at him." And to Weber in a still louder voice, as if he were addressing a child, "Why do you wear all those clothes?"

"He says he's cold," said Snow quietly.

"Yes, he's cold. I'm advising them upstairs, Weber, on account of you not bathing."

And Snow would have one more thing to say to Warden Buxton.

(Earlier, Keeper Kernahan, going off, had said to the chaplain concerning Weber, "Now he is like a baby. He wets his bed"—a needless comment, and it would be reported.)

Keough's inspection over, McDade in his cubicle, the condemned man said quietly, "I know I will fry like a fish alive in a pan."

"Did Kernahan say that to you?" Snow asked, furious.

"It don't matter who said it. The new electrician works for Westinghouse, and he wants to show how the dynamo is safe."

That was quite enough.

He went up to the warden's office and lodged informal complaints against Major Keough, Corporal Kernahan, and the convict barber. Then he went home for the book he had bought for Weber, thinking that here might be the answer, yet unsure until now—*No Darkness on the Deep,* it was called, a book about the science of electricity—and returned with it under his arm.

"I raised a subject the other day, do you recall, brother? We were talking about discovery, new worlds to be conquered, worlds in the very process of being won, the high excitement of it—of science and the work of scientists. Do you remember that I called these discoveries and inventions gifts to us? I have a book that will teach us something of these gifts."

There was to be no "moment" other than this. This was the moment.

"No, not a book of prayers, as you might think, Rupert. It is a book about the force of electricity. Look here."

After a moment, Weber took the volume Snow was holding out to him. It was new and expensive-looking with heavy marbled covers and a fragrant spine of leather, its title in gold, each page gold-edged. He opened it and an odor of ink filled the cage; the convict sniffed, his nostrils flared like a horse's. At last he thrust it back. "What about it?"

Snow, terribly excited, said, "I thought we might read in it."

8

The Romance of Electricity was its subtitle. Snow said it aloud and Weber stared, his bright eyes unwinking. He asked, "Is it a joke?"

"No," said Snow.

"Ain't I meant to laugh?"

McDade, hearing the altered tone, appeared from the cubicle.

"I supposed you was trying to joke with me," Weber said in a high angry voice. He was pale. "He has a book on the romance of electricity, McDade, and wants to read from it."

"Never mind, Rupert," Snow said. "I'll take it away then and won't bring it with me unless you wish me to."

He made as if to go, but turned. The pale convict was staring straight back at him. "You know you are called to amendment," Snow said urgently. "Make no error. This is a temptation put wickedly before you by men seeking personal advantage—this new talk of the lawyers. Resist it." He felt ill and dizzy; not

94

printer's ink but the effluvium of death, as if only now uncloseted, seemed to hang in the air between them. "I will help you if you let me. I implore you to let me, but you must attempt to resist these others."

9

Whereupon the condemned man swam away from him in rapidly reducing perspective, as if he were being whirled off in a wind; the bunk on which he sat crouched was one with the man this time, whirling and turning with him. The chaplain glanced down and saw without surprise that his hands were reduced too, hanging miles from him, tiny as birds' claws, the book like a chip in them.

"What's wrong?"

Dizzily, he sat on the bunk beside the other; he saw Keeper McDade, now the size of an insect, standing outside of the cage, swinging and catching a matchstick club. Weber had asked, "What's wrong?"!

". . . perfectly all right. One moment."

And then everything was all right, as he had said, and he was conscious of the convict's closeness, the sallow face near his, the thigh touching his. Not death—he smelled the man's soiled odor and an odor of woolens in summer: earthy and smoky.

"All right, padre?" asked McDade.

10

Recovered, energetic, springy as a bantam, he returned later; he apologized at once.

Weber said, "I got small."

"It happens within me. It is in my optic nerve—my brain and eye. But in fact nothing changes."

"Yet I got small, didn't I?" He made a gesture with his lean hands. "I don't like that."

With energy, Snow said, "I lie awake at night, like a child, in fear and trembling. I have a wife beside me, children near. Of course I know that God's world will lift me in the morning, that I will step out of doors, look around, breathe the air, and feel once more as if I am part of my own life. But at night I am entirely a foreigner in the earth; a fear that is cosmic grips me; you should know my mind dwells on you, and I'm afraid I will fail you; I am near dead with fear."

After a time Weber said, "Go on and read from that book if you want. I don't care."

11

In the late afternoon it grew dark. Soon it began to rain. Snow saw past Weber's profile silver streaks against the tree. The greenness of the soybean plants came fresh and powerful into the cage; smells of dung, green, and damped soil were almost palpable. He saw the condemned man shiver slightly inside his layers of clothing, looking and sniffing too. The minister thought: "He is feeling that it may 'go,' that it could be like the time before the reprieve when he was fearless."

12

Monotheism cleared the way: if it was not a brawny god hurling bolts of fire, then what in mischief was it? Another answer was needed.

Men had known of the existence of the force for twenty-five centuries; you did not see it, you saw what it could do. Snow brought in Mrs. Snow's amber beads and a few feathers, rubbed the beads briskly against his silk cravat, and watched Weber's surprised look as the beads fetched the feathers here and there. He wrote on Weber's slate and said, "That is the Greek word for amber, and it makes our word 'electric.' What do you think of that? And here are the beads themselves: 'brightness.'" Weber took them gingerly and gave them back after a moment.

The chaplain would arrive with the book in his hands. Though he already knew what was in it, he would open it with an air, keep a finger tucked in the place where he meant to read, and then introduce the subject with some simple figures. When the beads jerked the feathers toward them Weber could see the power of the electrically charged things. It was in the power, what it could do, that you saw the fluid. Weber would lie stretched out on his bunk, one leg flung over the other, a hand behind his head. Whenever Snow used unfamiliar terms, the convict would scowl: it was "Latin."

"Did he call your Greek Latin as well?" Dr. Clark asked.

"I think he is earnest. The hard part is getting into the subject." Weber responded in minute ways, ironically; yet the chaplain was not discouraged.

"It is a form of energy abroad in the atmosphere, Rupert, no more visible than the air. Yet, since you breathe it, you don't need to see the air to believe it exists."

Weber said wryly that he believed the electric was there, all right.

But did he? It was really, Snow saw, black mystery in the other's mind. There was nothing dark about that branch bending, he supposed. "It is wind doing its work: those leaves in constant motion, that cloud moving. But you can't see the wind, can you?" Well, as a matter of fact one could see electricity, which was more than could be said for brother wind: did Weber know when?

The condemned man looked livelier, as if he would give it some attention.

"You see it if there is an electrical storm at night, don't you, Rupert?—clouds grow thick with rain, large droplets charged with small, and they must discharge their electricity from cloud to cloud across the sky in bolts or into objects on the earth, and you see it against the dark heavens. Lightning! It is discharged electricity, channeled through the atmosphere—like a shot fired."

Weber smoked and stared up at the mesh ceiling of his cage. McDade hung near, listening with interest. It looked better now. The chaplain could tell he had the convict's attention. He brought in ebonite rods and pieces of metal and showed the other how the metal could be charged and then transfer its charge, share it with the second piece of metal; the metals conducted; the hard rubber insulated. Remove the insulation and the charge will go through the conductor and down into the earth. Watchful, Snow had Weber touch the electrically charged metal with a finger, and then when they tried to use the thing to attract a cylinder of paper it did not work. The weak electric charge had gone through Weber and into the earth.

"But there's more of it if it kills you," said Weber understanding.

All right: yes.

Weber nodded, blowing plumes of smoke.

". . . Alexander Volta, an Italian who died over fifty years ago. And a Signor Galvani, as well, from whose name the word 'galvanic' and the word 'galvanize,' referring to the results of studies in current electricity . . ." The whole matter of the nature of conduction: though Weber nodded solemnly, the chaplain saw that they had sailed into deep waters. Yet did it matter?

"That other is the one 'volts' comes from," said Weber.

Wasn't that the point, perhaps—that the condemned man was awake to him? All right. In that sense things could not have been going better.

"Benjamin Franklin . . ."

But Weber had never heard of Benjamin Franklin. For no reason he could fathom, this delighted Snow. He was ecstatic now in this moment of his life, in this prison chamber where, with knowledge, he would worry fear, worry death. Now there was light here, and these bonds that had already proved capable of developing between the men seemed potentially favorable: less prickly.

". . . the fluid lends itself to what is called 'conduction' along supple metal wires wrapped in insulation." It was another day. They had gotten farther along. "It goes through the wire and then back again, which is your alternating current, don't you know, switching constantly back and forth at one rate of speed or another, depending on the amount of pressure which has been generated. . . .

"A device called a 'commutator' converts the same fluid into one that will flow in a single direction only, and this is the direct current." He said watchfully, "The first is very powerful, and that is the one in this prison produced by Westinghouse's dynamo. The other is the method Mr. Edison favors, feeling it is safer in public works such as city lighting because it goes at lower voltages."

Weber, at ease on his bunk, nodded.

"Think of water going through an iron pipe," Snow started to go on: "Electricity in a wire is like that, and like water in a pipe its speed depends on the force with which it is pushed plus the size"—he made a circle of his thumbs and first fingers—"and what is called the resistance of the conductor through which it runs. . . ."

He stopped, knees weak. Without warning he had seen himself. And the sensation that followed was like one of weariness after a crisis; his burden of fear had that moment been abruptly removed, and he was exhausted and even angry, having lived so long with the burden and knowing it well. He had said nothing much different from other days on this one, but he had seen himself suddenly generative in the power of this beginning: seen himself as primary in it. And it was as if he had been flung componently for the moment from the self he had known, the components of him like those drops in Franklin's electrified jet of water, each repelling the other, so weary was he and relieved and shocked. Though he had planned to begin, set himself to it, and embarked upon the beginning, erecting the world in Weber, yet he had not *seen himself generative* in that world until this moment, and he was certain that he had been or was in the process of being freed entirely of all anxiety concerning the man Weber.

He had to sit down; and as he had the recent time he was ill he must sit down next to Weber.

"What?" The convict stared at the request, then slowly swung his legs over the edge of the bunk and made room. Snow sat beside him tired and irritable.

Their book was on the table out of reach. Propped against it was Weber's slate with Snow's diagram on it: A's attracting B's; A's repelling A's; B's repelling B's, attracting A's.

He remembered the moment later as the first true if one-sided engagement between them after their beginning.

13

In company with Buxton and Clark, Snow helped escort the State Commission on its quarterly tour of the asylum. Alexander, who had been one of Buxton's invited witnesses for the intended execution in April, was State Superintendent of Insane. When they opened the door to the chapel, the farther door of which led into the prison, so that it was common to both institutions, Alexander backed off with humorous haste. "Your countryside, pastor."

Snow was cheerful. "With a flock that is my captive as well as the State's. Few of my calling are so provided."

They looked into the kitchens and the bakery. Convict bakers, naked to the waist, slapped big ropes of dough onto a long marble table shaping them into loaves, then pushed them into the bread pans that were like troughs; the ovens roared; each commissioner ate a piece of fresh bread. Warden Buxton said in a joking tone; "What was the name of that play you and your people did, Hannibal? *The Last Loaf?* Perhaps this is it."

They were all cheerful, conscious of themselves. They smiled in the warm, delicious-smelling room, eating bread. Snow thought of Weber waiting for him. The bread was incredibly delicious in his mouth.

14

"How does our sacrifice to the electrical gods fare?"

The Commission wanted to see the chair. Since Buxton and the others were occupied, the job of guide fell to Snow, and he led them down. Cautiously, first Alexander, then the other two took turns sitting in it. They smiled in spite of themselves.

Weber stood with his long fingers hooked high into the mesh of his cage, seeming relaxed, at ease. As the visitors peeped in at him, he looked back with insolence that was nevertheless unaggressive.

As if he had only then thought of it, Alexander said, "As I'm here I might as well have a word with Mr. Weber."

He stood off from the cage and raised his voice. "How are you feeling?"

Weber gave a mild snort.

"Do you recognize me?"

"I don't."

"I am Dr. Alexander. We traded words on an earlier occasion concerning your feelings about the crime of which you have been convicted. Am I so unmemorable?"

Weber shrugged. Snow, standing to one side, gave him an encouraging smile. Alexander asked, "How do you sleep?"

"I think he sleeps very little," said Snow. "McDade?"

"The night man reports he don't sleep much."

"Let him answer, please. I want to ask you again, Weber, only to remind myself: what was the name of that young girl whose life you took?"

"What?" Weber half turned away. He looked shy. "Jenny?"

"That's right. I have an appalling memory too. Now, at this distance and under these circumstances"—with a gesture toward the death chamber behind him—"do you think that Jenny deserved what befell her: would you do it again, given the chance, if she angered you?"

"Well, I was drunk," said Weber in the shy tone.

"Given the chance you would not do it again, would you, Rupert?" Snow asked.

"No, I wouldn't," he replied to Snow.

"Please?" said Alexander, smiling.

"My trouble is I can't hold the drink."

"But, I suppose . . ."

". . . a rum-done, I was."

"Yet I suppose Jenny might have deserved what befell her—in your sense: she plagued you beyond endurance, as I remember it."

Snow protested; his face had turned angrily bright. "You understand that what you did was wrong, Rupert!"

Weber said, "Yes."

In private Alexander said amiably to the chaplain, "It's only that Buxton asked me to have a look at your man, because he felt that he might have become affected by his long-delayed sentence. My questions were intended to provoke him."

"Weber is all right in his mind."

The doctor was agreeable: "Well, you have had plenty of chance to observe him. He seems all right, does he? How is he taking the prospect of execution? He is not abnormally calm and resigned, is he? That would be odd."

"No, he is not. He is as I would expect him to be under the circumstances."

"I am told that he has wet his bed once or twice."

Snow was silent, exasperated.

"Well, I think pretty much as you do, after all, and I will say so to Buxton."

15

Snow was in the cage when McDade came on the next morning looking strange. The keeper nodded stiffly to the chaplain and ignored Kernahan. The night watch said something to him in an undertone.

"Never mind that."

Even from where he sat Snow smelled the spirits. McDade was stiffly formal in his movements. He did not look over at the chaplain. "Will you get his bucket, Kernahan?"

"It's empty."

McDade said, "Do you know poor Mrs. Buxton died in the night?"

Kernahan stared.

"She did."

Snow saw that Weber had heard; he would have told him in his own time, gently. He began, "It was very sudden . . ."

"Terrible. What was she—forty-five? Not that much," McDade was saying in a too-loud voice. He stood with his thick legs planted wide, head lowered. Kernahan waited, utterly still, shocked, the remains of his midnight meal wrapped up in a newspaper in his hand. "It's always the unexpected now, isn't it?" he said.

McDade kept clearing his throat.

"They could not diagnose her illness," said Snow quietly to Weber. He had been up since midnight, Buxton having sent for him as well as Dr. Baird. Clark had been there beside her bed, and toward morning the Syracuse physician, Widtman, came. "It is a great mystery still. There are few to match her spirit and her kindness. She was fond of you, Rupert."

Weber sat slouching on his bunk, his blue eyes ranging around the chamber, returning always to McDade.

"When she saw me she thought of you and asked about you."

Weber looked relaxed and contented. He asked, "Is your mother better?"

Kernahan went off. McDade went back and sat down, hawking his throat clear while Weber gave the keeper a shrewd lazy look. The chaplain replied, surprised, "She's stronger."

Weber nodded, looking shrewd. "Go on with it, then. About the electricity."

16

Keough came later with tobacco and a few kites. He was wretched-seeming, somehow undone, as if his uniform were incomplete. "Did you hear the news?" He kept sighing. "She will be sorely missed, I can tell you, sorely missed." He was as reluctant as a boy, unwilling to leave, attracted by the slow talk of disaster. McDade had emerged from his cubicle. Weber watched them. Once in a while one of the three would glance at him: Snow in his alert way, Keough surreptitious and oddly disheveled, McDade with his hung-over red-eyed passion. He looked calmly back at them all. At last he said, "Well, leave the kites and get out, Mr. Keough.

"Say, ain't you feeling well, Fred? I believe McDade is under the weather," he said, looking with shrewdness and sudden ferocity from one to the other.

Keough dropped the kites onto the keepers' desk and left, clattering up the iron staircase. Weber said casually, "Well, I guess I will take my exercise now."

17

He had not done so in more than three months. McDade fetched the shotgun and a chair from the cubicle, then let Weber out of the cage. Snow came out too with his book on electricity still in his hands and stood watching. It took him a moment to realize the significance of Weber's gesture. He said, "I'm delighted to see this, Rupert. Bravo!" But in fact the sight dismayed him.

McDade watched heavily. "Now he won't be so cold."

He walked up and down with long jerking strides, awkwardly raising his knees high. He glanced up at the light-filled window each time before he turned under it, took a breath, punched at his chest with the yellow fists, and exhaled noisily. He tried to touch his toes, but that appeared to make him dizzy. When he stood straight, swaying, eyes closed, to recover, Snow could see the pulses jump in the man's throat and temples. He said, "Don't overdo it, Rupert. Small steps first."

"Don't overdo it, Weber," said McDade.

Weber joked: "Then p'r'aps I'll do it over instead."

That night Snow said to his wife, "I cannot know what he feels about anything. It's hopeless. I expect all the wrong things. Of course, I am myself, not he, so how can I tell?"

She was amazed, as always, by his suffering and fearful of it. He suffered more these days than he ever had since she'd known him.

"Nor do I know at all what's wrong with me. I am myself, anyway! I was annoyed because he did not seem sorry for Mrs. Buxton. Annoyed! I saw that he fed on it. Then when I thought . . . saw that he could nourish himself on it, I grew rather pleased, or thought I was, as I had thought I would have been pleased to woo him with news of my own mother's death. But no: truly I was annoyed! Everyone is very strange—very! I'd give witness that Sergeant McDade came on duty this morning half intoxicated, which Weber did not fail to notice and feed upon too. That kind woman who pitied him! And I leaning over this way or that for his sake, utterly forgetting my duty. Don't I go to him now with a book of science and leave my Bible at home?"

She wondered why he could not admit that he was simply a good man trying to help another who was in pain.

"I? Well! No, if only I could talk to him! No, I don't know if I am reasonable myself. *He* has no intelligence for me to address. There, you see?—what I will say! I blame him for my failure. What's the matter?"

It made her weep.

They sat half hidden from each other in a glassed plant-porch, she with needlework forgotten in her lap. India-rubber trees in pots, palms, ferns crowded heavily around them. They stirred in the uncomfortable little sofa called a tête-à-tête, filled with anxiety. Each offered a hand and then dropped it. They stared through the dusk, each searching out the other's eyes.

She could only think after all that she would be afraid to see the man die. And it was unbearable to her, the thought of his seeing.

"No, it isn't terrible in that way."

Then he said in the darkness: "Here is what is terrible. It's as if one of us two in that death chamber were not a man at all, and Weber hastens to admit that he is not. It's entirely unacceptable, but there it is; he agrees to that to begin with: 'I am not a man like you'—as if he is saying, 'It's all right: kill me'—providing his own warrant, not to trouble us.

"Yet I own that we are making a start.

"I own that.

"'What am I? What does God require of me?' Not: 'It's all right. Kill me.' Not that.

"What have I got: three weeks?

"Poor Buxton is injured by his wife's death. Clark is cold. I am. So is Weber, and I utilize it meanly. We are brought down by the majestic occurrence when we ought to be raised: bowed down. . . . Now that we have made a start, now that I have his attention, I am not sure of anything. . . ."

But at dawn, alone on the street before his house, he was again exalted.

The perfectly clear gray sky promised a fine day. The earth held him familiarly to herself. The morning's first of the newly electrified Belt Line cars went ringing by downhill. It clattered with violent strength, discharging mechanical violence into the fresh July air, the operator in his cab both confident and intent, his raw-shaved face newly awake and clever, as wide awake as electricity, bright as the coming century. That was absolutely all right. It was as right as rain, as just and needful. Wasn't God's keen knowing on the dot in time and place? Oh, come: good! God was right here on the dot—inside him, outside, in that lean new electrical face in the incandescent streetcar at dawn—at dawn!

18

Reverend Baird said the service for Mrs. Buxton. The day had grown hot. They were gathered under a canopy set on poles. Snow watched his friend's face with its good lines. Buxton stood pale beside the coffin; Clark stood by with a bit of dirt and grass in his farmer's hand.

"Yet, O Lord God most holy, O Lord most mighty, O holy and most merciful Saviour, deliver us not into the bitter pains of eternal death."

Kernahan was there at the back of the little crowd, sun flashing from the handlebars of his Columbia that he had leaned against the palings before a monument. Over there against the cemetery's back road and out of sight was the quicklime pit for unclaimed dead from the prison. Weber would go into it. Why could not Snow, himself a minister of God, keep his attention upon a prayer for the eternal life of a woman whom he had loved? He watched Baird's lips move. A pair of dragonflies mounted one on the other flew into the green shade of the tent and out. On the dot! Kernahan, though in the sunlight, was something of a shadow where he stood with bowed head, an umbra in the July heat. " 'It would be strange indeed . . .' "

<h2 style="text-align:center">19</h2>

" 'It would be strange, indeed, if so readily controlled an agent as electricity, an Ariel before whom time and space seem to vanish, did not cross the threshold of our homes and enter into our household life. We find, in fact, that the adoption of electrical household appliances is daily becoming more widespread, here adding a utility, and there an ornament, until in the near future we may anticipate a period when its presence in the homestead will be indispensable. . . .' "

Weber looked thoughtful. The article in the magazine was illustrated: an electrical bell, an Edison telephone, a plan for wiring a house for the various appliances. When Snow passed the magazine to him he would look the drawing over carefully, pushing out his lips, nod, then pass it back still nodding, as if lost in working something out.

" 'The pressure of a finger on a button brings two strips of metal into contact and completes a circuit, forming as it were an electrical endless chain from the battery through the wires, the bell . . .' "

". . . completes the circuit."

"Exactly." And as for the strength to do the work: "In that case it's your electromagnet—the coiled wire we discussed?—which intensifies magnetic power sufficiently to lift the hammer that strikes the bell or, when a servant is required (I am not speaking of my household, Rupert), to release the room shutter in the annunciator system." Perhaps, with permission, Snow would bring in some material and together they could construct a simple buzzer.

The two methods: "Edison's requires a *little* intensification of power for home use. Westinghouse must use a transformer somewhere outside of the house to make the electricity safe inside. The latter is steadier, stronger, but perhaps not as safe."

"I get that now." He nodded. "I'm the one completes the circuit in there, ain't I?"

"A switch will do that. When the electrodes are fixed to your skin you will be part of an existing, still incomplete circuit, and the closed switch will complete it."

"I get that."

He was interested in Edison and listened closely when Snow spoke of him. The Wizard. He learned for the first time that Edison had been a witness at the hearings on his own case in the previous summer.

"So was Mr. Kennelly a witness who wrote this interesting article. He's Edison's chief electrician."

But the Wizard . . . He wanted to know if Edison had mentioned him by name at the hearings.

"I imagine he did. I am sure of it."

"And they were asking if this electric would work on me?"

"Edison knows that it will work very well indeed. Nobody of any standing in the field doubts it. Your lawyers say they do, but that is a legal attitude, not a scientific one."

The thoughtful nod from Weber.

". . . There will be thermostats to regulate and maintain household temperatures—even in summer, using ice-cooled air.

"According to Kennelly, there is a house near Greenwich, Connecticut, that has used ice-cooled air for the past two summers. You don't need that down here, do you, Rupert?" It was an interesting article, done in homely terms. Snow had already talked about the adventures of electrical science applied—stringing telegraph wires, the terrible rigors of laying a submarine cable to Europe, the complex telephone networks, city lighting, and tram systems, and the rest; he had described the great dynamos, the motors, and the motors' colossal work. . . . Now here in the article were the homely things, the plans for them like road maps or spiders' webs in boxes on the page. Snow waited, smiling, and Weber, as he had expected he would, joked: "I would break in and start that burglar alarm."

They sat side by side on the bunk to avoid passing the book back and forth, Weber looking over the chaplain's shoulder. "Who's that?"—a woodcut that showed a young man listening to an Edison phonograph: a tube grew from it and branched into the young man's ears; his lips were parted, eyes blind with listening.

"I don't think it's intended to be anyone in particular."

"The way they have him wired to it . . . I thought that was for the electrical execution—they would kill him with that box."

McDade had emerged and was observing them.

The author, Kennelly, recommended electricity in the billiard room to avoid soot and oil marring the baize, and suggested electric veranda lamps that would shine "heedless of the wind." "'. . . A very pretty effect can be also produced in conservatories, by suspending lamps of different colors half-hidden in the foliage.'"

The day watch snorted, and Snow came back amiably, "Never mind, Keeper. We are all right, I think, aren't we, Rupert?"

20

Two questions were uppermost in Weber's mind. Snow knew about the first—his wish that the action of the machine be swift: would it?—and they had discussed it openly, so that now the condemned man seemed confident upon the point; but he blamed himself for not having guessed the second. The convict dreaded mutilation, a change in the appearance of his dead body. The matter had been gone into during the hearings and after; whole articles had been written on the subject in scientific journals; yet

Weber in his cage, being told nothing, seeing no newspapers, knew less about this and other similar details of his celebrated case than any man in the street, and he had been shy about bringing it up. He went at it in a roundabout way. "Say, has that happened again where I get small?"

Not death, apparently, but any suggestion of an alteration in his physical self was dreadful. He got around to it. "It don't matter so much," he said, "yet I want to know."

"It has been taken into account. There is no risk at all, I am assured on the best authority, of any such effects." In fact it was one more of the many advantages of this technique over another.

Weber said, "Yes, hanging changes you. The sponges in the electrodes must be wet, though, ain't I right?"

"Yes, to lessen the resistance."

The convict seemed always willing to accept the other's assurances. He could sit beside Snow for as long as an hour at a time absorbed in study. Snow neglected nothing if the condemned man showed interest. If it was power plants or industry in the future, all right; if it was electrified railways, a technique to illuminate fountains at night, and Weber looked interested, the chaplain would go into them; and if it was the operation of the death chair, then that was all right too. He embarked on the troublesome matter of resistance to electric currents in animals and the function of the Wheatstone bridge in measuring it—"Yes, I get that"—but it was apparent that in physiology he had lost his man. It did not matter. He accepted the chaplain's word on it, pushing out his lips, nodding at the spidery drawings in the book. "All right." They were getting on. They spent an afternoon building the buzzer, which worked satisfactorily; they were easy with each other.

"Say, will that redheaded drink of water do it or the new man?"

"If you mean Mr. Stone, I understand that his contract is up. Your new man is Mr. T. M. Taggart."

"He won't play tag, I hope."

The convict's notion of humor:

"I wonder if I *ain't* out of my mind"—fixing the chaplain with a sallow straight stare. . . .

"Well, yes, but look at it: p'r'aps I am." This was a "touch." He was teasing, and he watched hard for a response. Snow would chew on his lip, look rueful, shake his head, then glance up sideways at the man who was going to die and smile; Weber would hold it a moment more, blue parrot's eye cold on the other, then wink. He might develop it:

"P'r'aps *you* are. What about that?"

Oh? The chaplain would have to give that one some examination.

"No, if I ain't, maybe you are. How about Fred?"

McDade, if he were there, would nod at it: "I often wonder."

"There! What about that? McDade's crazy too. I'm the only one who ain't!"

McDade listened to every word now between Snow and Weber; the new dialogues held his close attention. He was grave. He never smiled at the humorous exchanges. "I wonder if you couldn't make out a case on both of us," he would say, or something like it: "me and the chaplain"—looking at Snow.

In the controversy between Edison and Westinghouse, Weber was for the Wizard. "Westinghouse does not want his dynamo used in this," Snow said, "since he feels it is poor business. It's possible to understand that in my opinion. Edison declares that Mr. Westinghouse's dynamos and the alternating current are unsafe. As you know, there have been a number of accidents due to high-tension wires falling into the streets, and other causes—more than a hundred deaths so far—so that people feel the wires and cables should be underground. But Edison feels even that is unsafe, and that no sort of insulation is perfectly capable of protecting the public from the alternating current. It's his wish that continuous current be substituted for it. He says it's the only safe way."

Weber nodded. But McDade, standing outside of the cage, snorted. "Yes, that's why the Wizard got Stone to put this machine in here. To show the world it is unsafe."

Weber joked, at ease on his bunk: "It won't be safe for me."

"Isn't it a coincidence," said McDade, "that Mr. Edison is trying to make a living selling continuous and without success, and that Mr. Westinghouse is getting rich with his alternating?"

"Edison is interested in the public safety," said Snow.

Weber nodded. The keeper looked at him.

"Go on, Fred. What are you looking at?" asked the convict.

McDade said, "Edison is interested solely in his pocketbook, like any one of your industrial tycoons."

"Go on," said Weber. "The Wizard is all right."

21

But if the chaplain mentioned the name of God, Weber backed up at once as before, a stoat dark in a dark corner of his box: sullen, hunched, secret, undeclared. Scenting Snow's intent before it ought to have been apparent, before it was apparent even to the other, weasel-like, Weber backed rapidly off from God and shut himself down; he shut himself off like the closing of an eye: "I tried it. It don't go." Snow saw how it was possible to help with Weber's trick and do no more than that: stop short, serve pride, and fail God.

22

When Warden Buxton came down to the cage the morning after the funeral Snow whispered to the convict, "I wish you would say something, Rupert."

"What about?"

Keough was with the warden. "Tobacco, young feller my lad,"

he said heartily; he kept casting worried glances at Buxton. "The smokin's."

"Good morning, Snow," Buxton said. "How are you, Rupert?" Snow had risen. Weber remained sprawled over his bunk.

"I'm all right," the convict said loudly, insolently.

Buxton looked just as usual. He signaled to McDade to open the cage. Weber rolled his first cigarette, took the keeper's light, and lay down again on the bunk. While Keough made his inspection Buxton had McDade open the other cage; he wore a black silk ribbon around the arm of his coat, his silver hair shone, and he moved energetically. His eyes, Snow noticed, were particularly clear, as if death had cleared them. He was mild, intent, busy. Snow pitied him: how stiff he kept his back! He bent stiffly to look under the unmade bunk in the empty cage and grunted rising. He came out and gazed thoughtfully at Weber.

Keough said, "The murderer Fisch is coming here from Sing Sing tomorrow night or the following morning. You and him should be good friends, Weber. I suppose you don't know what he done."

"No."

"I suppose you want to know. Well, he shot a man in a saloon in New York. That's all."

"It will be company for you," said the warden.

A mat hung from the ceiling beam between the cages. "How can I see him?"

The warden was gazing at Weber in that oddly still, clear-eyed way. Snow saw Weber become conscious of the stare. Buxton raised his hand slightly. Removed, from out of his dream the warden murmured, "We must do it."

Chaplain Snow went upstairs with him. The warden said, "Did you want to see me?"

A man from one of the press associations was in the ante-office, and Snow waited while Buxton spoke to him. Then he said, "I apologize for Rupert's behavior."

114

"No need."

"It has grown so damp and hot here. Couldn't you go away for a few days?"

"Clark thinks you need a rest yourself."

He went through some of the papers on his desk. His clerk, a safety, was talking to two visitors in the corridor outside. Buxton said, "Well, I will stay on for now. I have written to the Governor and Superintendent of Prisons asking them to accept my resignation as of the end of the third quarter. I am not telling everyone."

"What will you do?"

"I don't know." Then he said, "I'm told that you really do discuss electricity with Weber."

When he tried to explain himself again he felt that Buxton was not listening. There would be no good time now to raise difficult subjects with him. He said something about McDade almost casually.

"Do you know that for certain?"

"He certainly appears to be intoxicated. Weber jokes about it. And Corporal Kernahan is little better, though he does not drink."

Buxton said suddenly loud, "I must say it is very pleasant to have such items dropped into my lap just now! What else have you got for me?" And then: "McDade is crackajack with the condemned. Grand."

In a moment he said more quietly, "Mrs. Buxton could not bear the thought of his being killed."

He said, "If it happens again with the keeper, let me know."

And in another moment, veering once more, he apologized to the chaplain. "I'm sorry. I will try to find time to see about McDade, Hannibal."

23

The boy Carpenter was still with them. He looked wan because he missed his mother, and Snow had difficulty with him.

He proposed walks and fishing excursions to the lake, but the boy was not interested. Once they tramped out to visit the prison barns a mile or so distant from the minister's house, and Carpenter looked listlessly at the big-uddered cows and Clydesdales with their hoofs as large as peach baskets. He did not much like animals though, apparently. Snow thought boys should act like boys; his girls were very like girls. He did not know what to make of a quiet listless boy. It was not as if the chaplain enjoyed fishing and hiking and cycling himself; in fact any exercise more strenuous than a sedate stroll put him out of sorts. He had, before he was thirty, become a man who liked a good companion and a vista, a stroll, interesting conversation that was not theological for preference, since he believed in trying to keep a clear division of work and recreation. It never occurred to him that his nephew might be the same. As a result there was antagonism between them.

"It's likely you'll want to climb up into that loft."

Another boy would be up the ladder like a monkey to jump into the sweet-smelling hay, but Carpenter shook his head. They were both scarlet with heat; bits of dry seed and farm dust had stuck to their foreheads and got under their collars. Snow poked here and there with his stick, thinking of his affairs, and forgot the boy.

"What's wrong with this cow, Uncle?"

He peered through a trap at his feet. The boy had gone down into the cattle stalls again and was staring at a barrel-ribbed Jersey with knock-knees who moaned, thrusting up her wet snout.

"She is going to have a calf."

"Oh." The boy asked, "Where does it come out?"

Snow said, "There under her tail," resolutely.

"It's dirty."

"She does better if she's left alone. We'll go look at the hogs and goats."

Carpenter said something inaudible beside the goat pens.

"What's that?"

"I want to go home to my own house."

"As soon as Grandmother is well enough. Are you so tired of us?"

The boy frowned at the self-gratifying question, and Snow said, "Of course, you miss your mother and your companions, don't you?"

They were both tired by now, and the walk back loomed. Carpenter kept complaining that one of his legs was strained and that he could not walk. He stopped every few feet.

Then, out of the blue, he asked, "Why are you going to kill that man?"

"What?"

"You are going to tie wires to him and kill him with electricity." He had stopped once more and was rubbing his knee and staring at the dark prison towers on the horizon and at the brick and stone town beyond, which was like a piece of the sky. They had passed a road camp—mules pulling wagons full of crushed stone, convicts marching lockstep: grinning secret men—and Carpenter had hurried by, looking arrogant in his terror, chin in the air.

"You mean Weber?"

"Is that his name? Belle told me you're going to kill him."

"I am not going to do it personally," said Snow, upset. Belle told him! "The law has convicted Weber of taking someone's life, of doing it wittingly. The State of New York has imposed this penalty and will carry it out."

"What difference does it make who does it?" the boy returned in his arguing way. "Will you watch?"

"Yes. To help him."

Snow asked, "Were those Belle's words to you?"

"No, no," his nephew said impatiently. "They're my words." He was pale, the corners of his mouth white. "I'm going to have a movement."

There was a screen of weeds on the edge of the road, and

Carpenter went there and squatted palely with his trousers down; then he was sick instead. Snow did not know what to do. The boy waved him away. Snow supposed he saw him killing a man, wrenching the life from him as if it were a bad tooth.

24

Your time draws nigh,
So does mine.
All God's work must die.
What use to pine
Or what to sigh?
All mere men must die.
He's waiting there and by and by
He'll lay it on the line—
"Say, Weber, look about and see
Why all my work must die.
In Happy Isles I wait for thee!
To Live my work must die!"

The barber had come late. Snow, as he descended the stairs into the basement chamber, heard his loud stressing voice.

"And I will fry!" shouted the convict, gasping with laughter. McDade guffawed, invisible in his cubicle, and the barber Stern spun in a circle on one foot, laughing. "That's it! You're game, Weber! Wait till the boys hear that one! You're a trump!"

Weber saw the chaplain but did not change his tone. "Say, Fred, ain't you supposed to guard me here? What if I take Stern's razor off him?"

The odor of whiskey was powerful. It seemed to come from everywhere. Weber's face had been scratched: long bloody lines on his forehead and cheeks.

"Well, will you?" McDade rumbled.

"P'r'aps." Stern had seen Snow and was packing up his tackle. Now McDade came rather quickly out of the cubicle and stood planted, flipping the weighted stick up into his broad palm and letting it go. He grinned. "Good morning, Chaplain." His eyes were congested.

"Have you had liquor, Rupert?"

"No."

"You must tell me." The barber left, and Snow went into the cage. "You stink of it!"

"I gave him a nip of it, Mr. Snow," McDade said.

"Did you? Did you?"

"I came on with it. See his face. Kernahan said he had nightmares and scratched himself that way."

"And so you thought you would give him a drink and have a few yourself."

"Yes, sir." The keeper stood firmly planted; he seemed composed; the breath whistled calmly through his nostrils. Snow did not really know how to go on. Did the man want to lose his job?

"Dr. Clark will want to look at those," he said at last to Weber. The condemned man smirked. "Or is it quite all right?" He was becoming annoyed.

Weber, smirking, said, "You don't care."

"I do." And then, in an altered tone, lowering his voice, "I do, Rupert. Indeed I do. What wouldn't I do to show you?—my love and God's. He is so patient and loving! Won't you look up at Him again?"

McDade said, "I washed them off for him. He don't want the doctor."

Weber was staring down at the floor; he shook his head, smirking.

"*Why* won't you?" asked Snow.

It irritated Snow to see McDade's great red face there. It put him in a passion of irritation! Weren't there enough constraints? "I am afraid to mention God's name to you! I have no other job in the world but to laud His name, yet you prevent me; rather, I am constrained here! It beats me absolutely what I am to do!" Of course, he must simply get down onto his knees. Pride prevented it, not Weber: pride of the subtlest, most treacherous sort prevented him, pride in his own intellect and its hunger to find an intellect in others, even in Weber. Not McDade, drunk, goggling at them, but his own pride like a hook in him held him up on his feet. Yes, it was all his prideful notion of starting from scratch with first things, of being himself primary rather than God, of "creating bonds" where all-sufficient bonds already existed between Weber and his Maker, of being himself more than a plain road; he could not be satisfied to be what he had signed on to be—the bearer of good news—and so he was, of course, less than that. He was too young. He did not, really, know a thing about death—Mrs. Buxton's was the first he had witnessed, and he had been like ice about it, wanting only to utilize it—and the one thing he really *knew* about God now was that he had pretty well better get down onto his knees, *quick*, before it was too late!

In a flat rude voice Weber said, "It's all bull-cock." And then: "Sorry."

"Rupert . . ."

"Never mind," he said, vaguely maudlin. "I am sorry."

Snow reached out. Weber grasped the young man's neat hand, and for a moment they hung together, positively, consciously joined. Snow's heart pounded high. There was Weber's little smile offered. But still the chaplain did not pray, silently or aloud; he did not bend his knees. McDade looked calmly on; he might be in the theater. Snow thought: "He is only drunk. They are both drunk." His mind kept flying from this joining, so he could not understand it. And suddenly the offered hand was not a good gesture. Weber kept pumping his arm, squeezing Snow's fingers in a kind of spasm; the convict's hand was hot and dry as if he burned with fever; he held one hand under the chaplain's elbow and nervously squeezed and pumped with the other like an office-seeker at a picnic. McDade watched stolidly. Weber's smirk behind the bloody scratches had become a sallow insulting grin. Snow could not rid himself of the hand. Was he being made fun of? There had been a moment like this, now driven from memory so that only its outline was left: someone in a house that was like a gutter and someone else holding his hand, smirking: a witless, deadly benediction. He pulled himself free of the condemned man but kept his anger for the day keeper. "You need not stay, Sergeant. This time is no different from any other. We are all right alone."

McDade, red-eyed, would not budge.

"Go on with the electricity. Don't mind Fred. He's a rum-done."

Snow had promised to bring in Edison's testimony, and he had it with him. Perhaps what he felt himself now was a sort of moral drunkenness. Alternatively, what *were* the deserts into which one plunged to find one's sheep if not stony and terrible?

25

"That will do," said McDade.

Weber waved to the keeper to be silent. Snow went doggedly on with it. McDade's face was red. "Why are you reading him that? What use is it? We are not supposed to read the news stories to him."

"This is from the records of the court. It is Mr. Edison's testimony."

"That where he talks about burning—that the current would carbonize a man . . ."

"It is Bush trying to trip him up." He shuffled back through the loose-leaf pages. "Edison says—here it is: 'I don't understand that. I don't understand how it would be possible.' If you please, now . . ."

"What good are you doing here with this? Weber don't understand. . . ."

"Warden Buxton knows . . ."

"What—that you talk about burning men up?"

"It is Mr. Bush in court. . . ."

"What the hell do I care who? Or Weber? Aren't you supposed to bring the comfort of God? What the hell sort of a parson are you?"

"It is testimony before the State . . ."

"Oh, my eye!"

Weber grinned.

"Come, Parson, I hear you reading this, which is against every rule, and I listen to the cant—the scientific hogwash. Your Edison is only a brute. . . ."

Snow read across this from the testimony in a sharply raised voice: " *'Now you were asked* what current would be necessary . . . *what current would be necessary* for Mr. Weber, or anybody else, and you said about 1,000 volts. . . .' "

"Now isn't *that* enough? Right there!"

Snow rose, his fair cheeks flaming, bounced up from the bunk on which he had been sitting next to Weber. "I know what I am doing! You are drunk! You go to work and corrupt—*corrupt* my man, undo my work! You have admitted you gave him whiskey. . . ."

"Go on. I want to hear," the condemned man shouted through this, grinning. The raised voices sounded like drums in the subchamber. "Didn't he say my name then? Didn't he say 'Weber'?"

". . . gave him comfort, which is more than you're up to! . . . this suffering man—look at his face! Can't you bring a bit of peace with you instead of guff about your sanctified Mr. Edison? . . ."

". . . quite enough, quite enough!"

"Not half enough!"

"Rupert, I suppose you could not hear what I read?" His temper lost, he repeated Bush's question from the testimony in a loud voice; McDade, then Weber each interrupted in loud overriding voices, through which Snow's cut shrilly: "*Answer:* 'With the average resistance of the body a thousand volts would give about an ampere, and *I think that is about ten times more than is necessary!*' "—shouting.

"Don't they have there how Edison got Stone his job as State executioner to use the alternating?"

"As a matter of fact, there is something . . ."

"Well, isn't he a hell of a witness—the devil's witness? I'll tell you what it is, Weber, and you listen to me!" shouted McDade, standing outside of the cage, banging his stick against it for emphasis. "There's a pair of knaves for you—that Edison and that Westinghouse. Now, here it is! Don't think they give a damn for you, for they don't! Their sales figures absorb all their interest. Are you glad your name was on Edison's exalted lips? Let me tell you that it isn't humanity that prompts him in this, Weber. It's money! Your quick death represents money to him! And the other fellow—your other humanitarian there—would save you to make his money—or keep from losing it, which is what hurts more! That first fellow in here: very well: Edison put him in. He *put him in!* And this other gent—Taggart: what about him? Yes, well never mind. Never mind now. Parson, setting your science aside, just see to 'your man' and his peace of soul and don't sell him Edison or the other! What sort of *fool* do they suppose a fellow is not to see their reasons! They are all bastards, every one! I am sorry, Weber. I'm sorry. I am drunker than I look."

"Indeed you are not. *I* will see that you are discharged at once."

"Yes, all right, Chaplain. It's what I want. I suppose you will, and that's what I want, for I can't bear this any longer"—gesturing at Weber. His voice was quieter. "That will suit me. You're a good enough man, Snow. I suppose I see what you're after here, but it's no good. Weber won't see it. And the world being what it is on the one hand and the State what it is on the other, well, you had better not rely upon anything but God to help this young man."

"In fact I do not . . ."

"That's all right. Yes, I am drunk. You tell Mr. Buxton that McDade came on drunk, brought a bottle and gave a drink to poor Weber. If you don't tell him, I will, for I've had all I want of it down here. You listen to me, Weber. If you can't contrive it with God, then you rely upon yourself—get right inside yourself and learn how to act out your courage, whether you feel it or not, and that will make it possible for you; but what you don't want to do is rely on anyone else—not on one of them: Edison, nor Westinghouse, nor Mr. Snow here, nor even McDade, not upon anyone but yourself; for when you really want one of us bad, we'll likely be off somewhere else whistling up other game and will have forgotten you."

"That is quite enough."

"It isn't half," said the keeper, swaying.

"You're wrong on the Wizard, Fred," said Weber.

"Don't rely on it. Nor on your electrical parson here. You talk about your trick. Right. Well, don't rely on us to help if you can't on God. Act it out. That's all you can do."

Abruptly, awkwardly, he turned back into his cubicle. Snow heard his heavy breathing and sighs. He said nothing.

"Go on with it."

"I will." But he was still silent.

Weber said at length in a raw, rather guilty tone, "You know, he gave me a drink. He ain't fit for this work, is he?"

Snow felt disarmed. What did he know? Bitterly: he knew nothing about drunkenness and life, sobriety or the grave; he knew nothing about men, nothing. Was McDade so far off the mark? He could understand almost anything; but he knew almost nothing. Nothing. The single thing that was right to do he could not do on this morning: he could not bend his knees.

In his new, lively excitement, Weber was scratching himself, his hand at his crotch rubbing; he was unconscious of what his hand was doing. "He ain't fit to do it," he was saying in a low informer's tone. "Did you hear him—all he said?"

26

Warden Buxton and Keough brought the new prisoner down. The man was small and fair with a roundish face. He kept his face turned away and his head lowered; there was a little bald patch on the top of his head. Weber sat casually on his bunk, a knee raised, a hand dangling over it.

"Rupert," Buxton said, "here is company for you."

The man stood between his warders, head hanging down. Keough carried his belongings—a canvas valise, a few books tied with twine, a banjo. Snow had spoken to Buxton, and McDade had been sent off earlier, though not yet officially suspended. The guard put on to replace him opened the other cage and stood by, rocking up on the balls of his feet, the shotgun, which both Kernahan and McDade usually left in the cubicle, across his arms.

"Here is the famous Rupert Weber," said Keough.

Snow stood beside the new man. Weber looked him over coolly; Fisch neither spoke nor raised his head. "You will find yourself comfortable enough," said the principal keeper to him. "It's the quietest spot in prison, barring the jails, and you ought to get plenty of nod. The food is first-rate too. Hearn likes it; don't you, Hearn?" he said loudly to the new young guard.

"In a sort of way, sir."

Keough rummaged around in the other cage, patting the bunk, looking for dust. "Quiet and cool," he was saying. "Cool and quiet. Too quiet for Weber. It's been too quiet for you, Weber, hasn't it?" he called. "Well, now you have a mate." When he said he was ready, Fisch turned and shuffled obediently into the cage before Hearn, his small feet pigeontoed in prison slippers. Buxton lingered near Weber, red-eyed, looking worn.

"Mrs. Buxton told me she used to read to you from this,

Rupert." It was *The Life of Duty.* "I believe she would want you to have it on your table."

Weber glanced at the book; he shrugged.

"She spoke of you often. It was her wish for me to serve you as well as possible." He kept shifting the small blue and gold volume from one hand to the other. "I do not blame you for what happened this morning; neither, I think, does Mr. Snow—am I right, Hannibal?—for your taking a drink. I hardly blame Sergeant McDade, who is getting old. It seems that his emotions overwhelm him."

"McDade ain't fit."

"Perhaps not. I hope Hearn treats you with friendliness. I want you to tell me if he doesn't."

Keough came out of the other cage.

"Have you got Weber's tobacco?" Buxton asked. "Give it to me. I'll find you in the mess hall, Major. You stay, Snow."

He waited until Keough had banged with his cane up the iron stairs and Hearn had returned to his cubicle, then passed the tobacco through the mesh. He had an air of uncertainty, of loitering.

"Can't you give me a light?" Weber demanded.

Then he blew long plumes at the ceiling.

Buxton said, "If you want to keep from scratching yourself like that in your sleep, we can have bandages put on your fingers. No? I see that you no longer wear such a lot of clothing."

"I ain't so cold."

Buxton nodded. "It is not inconceivable," he said, "that if you felt very unwell—I mean to say unstable—your case might bear a review. Do you understand? It isn't always the fact that a victim of mental sickness knows he is so. The reverse is usually true, and the fellow who is mentally—I am unfamiliar with alienists' terms . . . is the one to insist that he is well, though that is no reliable symptom either. In any event, it appears to me and others who watch that you are less well than you ought to be even under these very difficult circumstances." He glanced at Snow. "You see, I say this before you, Hannibal."

Weber said, "I ain't crazy."

"I don't suggest . . ."

"But you say maybe I am if I claim I ain't."

"I say it may be in my power to get a stay from Governor Hill if you are; but not, as I think you well understand, without evidence. There is pressure upon me from men like Fox and others, and I am urged to complete this job without delay. They are very hot on the subject. A further stay would make an uproar in the press, and I would be accused of collusion, as I have been before now—that is, of entering into secret, even illegal pacts in what is by law a public matter." He spoke so low that Snow could barely hear, yet the minister was certain he was meant to. "I am already accused of siding with Westinghouse in the electrical companies' controversy. I don't know how much Snow has told you about it. . . ."

"I'm for Edison."

"Yes. Well, in any event, perhaps you can see that one more delay, review, and possibly a commutation would make me out very dark indeed. It's likely I would be denied public employment afterward. I don't know. But whatever may happen—this is what I wish to make clear—I am more than willing to risk it. I will risk it gladly if there is the smallest chance that your mental state is abnormal. I must say that I do not want you killed by that machine."

"I'm to act out I'm crazy."

"No. Indeed you are not. I suggest no such thing. But there is no reason to be at pains to hide symptoms if they occur. Dr. Clark knows this. I hope you do too, Hannibal."

Snow said nothing.

"If the machine ain't used to kill me, then you'll scrag me, right?" Weber gave his little gasp of laughter.

"The law provides for electrical execution only. And with insanity fairly established, you'd be commuted—put across the wall into the asylum."

"What about this other bird you just brought down?"

Buxton made a gesture; it was as if he had said, "That is another matter."

When the warden had gone, Snow said, "I will come and talk to you in a moment, Rupert." He went into the new man's cage and sat on the three-legged stool there. The man kept his head lowered. He perched on the very edge of his bunk, feet together, head bowed nearly to his knees. He lifted it a bit when Snow addressed him, and dropped it again. The minister could get nothing out of him. There was a Bible among the books on the table and some religious tracts. Snow composed himself, covered his eyes, and prayed for this man—the murderer Fisch. After a time he heard Weber's voice muffled from the other side of the mat: "I want my exercise, screw."

The convict's tone was irritable.

He heard him stamping up and down the chamber then, taking deep breaths and blowing them out noisily. He saw Hearn on his tilted-back chair, the gun across his knees, turn his head back and forth like a man at a tennis game, watching Weber. The young guard had a look of power; his black crisp hair grew into a blunt point low on his forehead; his beard was heavy, though shaved close; his hands were so big that the old sawed-off shotgun was a toy in them.

Snow saw that Fisch had raised his head and was looking at him. Immediately he went to sit beside him. "I have just prayed. Will you pray with me, brother?"

The man stared at him.

"Shall I call you Jack? Do you mind?"

There was Weber peering irritably into the cage, flapping his thin arms across his chest. "Ain't you coming to see me?"

Snow held up a finger: in a moment.

"Well, you will find I am at home."

Hearn had risen. "Come on, Weber."

"You're fond of that gun, ain't you? Does it make you brave?"

The minister heard him locking Weber up again; he heard him say calmly, "Yes, like your ax made you, Weber."

"Yes, all right! Never mind!"

When Snow came to Weber at last, the condemned man said testily, "I don't want you. You can go. None of that will go for me"—with a wave at the other cage. "Goodbye, toodle-oo."

27

Snow was careful in his sermons to the insane, as if he were talking to children. The July heat upset them and knowledge of the coming executions, which there was no way of keeping from them.

". . . What did I observe this morning as I walked to meet you? Didn't I see birds and hear their song? They stay a bit, give us a tune to cheer us, then off into the blue. Our spirits will rise just so, we may perceive, like the birds. Our spirits are birds pining to be released to fly straight up into heaven. Look out at the blue sky! Yes, do look now. Now what? Go ahead, sit on the floor if you like. Look, I will sit with you. . . . Well, let me try to tell you what else I noticed. Have I said flowers? You have the same ones I observed in beds under these windows and in the flower boxes you tend. Can't you smell them? Can't you? I can. That's right. We have roses from God to cheer us, haven't we? They are the words of God too, for He does not always speak as we are speaking now. When He wants to be very clear and straight He does, men; when there are laws He needs to set forth, for example, and He wants to be quite clear about them.

"Well, let me think.

"Yes! I saw my children this morning too, and they are another sort of flower, aren't they?—a message from God saying rather urgently, 'Thus ye must become.' Everywhere, everywhere about us are His gentle, yet urgent messages, His telegrams of love: 'Come home. Father misses you.' Am I not right? Does that ring the bell? 'Father misses you. He forgives all.' He means you, and He means me. We are wanted, sorely missed, deeply loved, our transgressions *entirely forgiven,* our future joy utterly assured.

"Well. Would you like me to tell you a story at this time? You say when you are tired of it, and I will stop. . . . Don't you know that in olden days everyone was greatly desirous to hear our Lord speak in actual words, in their tongue, and visibly, not with children and flowers, Himself invisible; and that was it: they wanted to hear Him and see Him too. It was why the son of God came down to them, wasn't it? To be manifest? All right. He did. And He died for us and took away all our sins. All right. Now, that's not the story yet. Just suppose that the Lord had come into town here and you were allowed to leave this poor place to do it: wouldn't you run to hear Him speak? You'd flock to Him, am I not right? And then, once in the hall, well, wouldn't you know it, there'd be some people—not you; we will call them Pharisees: empty people who observe the form rather than the content of Christianity—well, wouldn't they, seeing you from the prison, from the asylum, wouldn't they *murmur?* Well, they would! And the scribes would too. Does it ring a bell? The old men set in their ways, our scribes: shall I call them the judges and lawyers? . . . Yes, it makes you laugh. And we are getting a little murmuring here, aren't we? Is that you, Jim Collins? All right! And Patrick. Well, you two lads just simmer down if you please!"

But the disturbance grew. Men began to overturn their stools, which were not, in the chapel, fixed. Some kept waving at Snow where he sat on the edge of the little stage, and he waved back. His eyes danced alertly here and there; he kept his small elastic body tense. The asylum guards moved in vigorous strides from one spot to another in the chapel. Only an hour before he had delivered the same sermon to the asylum women, and that had gone off well.

Snow tried a new beginning. " 'And he said . . .' "

Hopeless.

" *'A certain man had two sons . . . !'* "

Now and then a guard caught the chaplain's eye and gave a meaningful shrug. Snow would nod in return and smile slightly. He waited. It was a mystery to him how they knew: the day, the hour, details that were kept carefully secret. When he asked directly, they would know nothing. State Superintendent Alexander had warned him to suspend Sunday services in the asylum until Weber was dead or at least until there was some relief from the heat. They were unmanageable. A man turned smiling under a window in the sun, eyes closed. Some hid terrified under their chairs. The usual few at the rear sat as if drugged, heads lolling, arms hanging. The guards, with Snow looking on, were gentle enough, yet he winced watching them work. The man Collins had begun to fight. He had his arms pinned behind him by one guard and his head pulled back by the hair by another. Snow knew nearly all of them by name, knew where they were born, what their crimes and terms were, and when they had been transferred to the asylum. He stopped trying to speak. Now and then he would return a wave.

On Sunday afternoon a chapel entertainment, arranged by Snow for those inmates Keough passed, was given by Casey's Cornet Band of the town, followed by a literary performance: Misses Alice Maud White, Caroline Wheeler, and Jessie Kosters —a playlet, poems, and concert recitation:

"Look not mournfully into the *past*; it comes not back again. Wisely improve the *present*; it is thine. Go forth to meet the shadowy *future* without fear and with a manly heart. . . ."

Snow said a few words, after thanking the performers. He read from a letter written by an ex-convict now working in New York City, careful to avoid the parts that praised him. " 'A brother is someone who knows all about you and loves you just the same.' "

Snow was asked by Buxton to suspend Sabbath services until the dog days were finished.

"I would rather not. The services are important just now."

"I will give you the signal when you may resume them."

It was very frustrating. The two men were stiff with each other. A table from Dr. Alexander's annual report was on the desk, and Buxton asked the minister to glance at it. Under "Exciting Causes of Insanity" were items such as "blow on the head," "business trouble," "enormity of crime," "fear of punishment," "heart disease and masturbation," "heredity," "masturbation and excess of tobacco," "fit of anger" . . .

It was nonsense.

Snow said humorously, "I may just have a fit of anger myself." And then: "I wish you would not suspend my Sundays with the men."

"Continue your discussion groups."

The two looked at each other angrily across the desk. Buxton slept in the prison now, in an apartment adjoining his offices; his lights were seen from the yard to burn all night.

"Do you think these causes are ridiculous, Mr. Snow?"

"Weber is not insane."

"Then you know more than the experts. They are not sure. And you know everything about electricity too."

"Certainly not . . ."

He was to confine his final talks with Weber to spiritual matters. "I will ask the new day man to tell me if you don't."

"As your agent . . ."

"He is not my agent. It was you asked me to take McDade off."

"You must not tell me how to deal with Rupert."

"Yes, you are doing your best."

Buxton was pale with anger and exhaustion. The man's grief disarmed Snow, yet he was angry too, and he fought for what was necessary and right. As if to test his own integrity, he asked once more at this worst possible moment, "*May* I not have back my Sundays with all the men?" challengingly.

29

He looked over the outgoing prison correspondence in his own office—it was heaviest on Sundays—and a few of the illegal kites that had been routed across his desk. The work calmed him.

There was a kite addressed to Weber:

Hello! *Now!*
I say unto thee today, 'Thou art now with me in hell,' Ps. 9, 17—and so are all thy conspiring murderers, practising for their own damnation, obeying—in spite of themselves and their rebellion.
LEWIS THE LIGHT.
Accuser and Avenger. Note my acts 3.23—13.41.
Rev. 1.18—19.15—22, 12, 13, 16.
The Electrocutor of the World.

Here was insanity, if you liked. He supposed he knew the man who had written it and made a note to talk to Clark about him. *I Jesus have sent mine angel to testify unto you these things in the churches. I am the root and the offspring of David and the bright and morning star.* Both he and "the electrocutor of the world," Snow supposed, could know these words with safety, since God would arrive on the dot for both.

Calmer, he visited the hospital. No one was very sick in spite of the heat; and in fact a breeze had come up and was moving out some of the stale prison air, bringing the scents of a summer evening in its place. The pre-lights-out clamor had begun. Snow walked up on the galleries. Unlike other administration, the young minister was greeted cheerfully; and he would pause at one or another of the heavy iron-lattice doors, put his face close or push in a finger to be shaken. Occasionally there would be a gift for him or his wife or the girls—a work basket, a pencil box, a doll—waiting on the high slops shelf outside a cell: an individual's gift or one from a whole gallery. This time there was a set of dominoes in miniature fitted into a tiny box, and when Snow tried to thank them, a cheer was raised from a dozen cells so that he could not. . . . Ritually, first of all, his health and his family's were asked after at each grate.

"We are all very well."

"Don't he sound tired, though?"

"Well, I am a little, perhaps. . . ." He gave them a confidence. "I am disappointed. My services have been suspended because of the dust raised in chapel this morning."

They were sympathetic. "The poor kinks are working up to Weber's paying his debt to society."

"Which is why I need the meetings: to explain and to quiet them."

"I'll endorse it with the warden, Mr. Snow. We're old friends."

Most of them wanted to know about Weber's state of mind.

"All right, really. He stays very contented for the most part. I am sure he is not afraid."

To Wilson, with whom he had particular sympathy, he said low, "I don't know at all, Matt. I am not getting through to him, and the new man being there seems to make it worse instead of better."

"Ask Buxton to move Fisch."

"There ought to be mutual comfort."

"In principle . . ."

"Well, we'll see. Your advice is usually reliable, Matt."

He moved up and down the walks, climbing steel stairs from one gallery to the next. Instead of falling silent as they did during other inspections, the prisoners, hearing his steps, called to him. "Stop here, Mr. Snow?"

"I want a word with you."

"Stop here, Mr. Snow. I have something that may just interest you."

And this night someone shouted with pleasure, "It's snow! Snow in July!"

30

Then the summer bore down. Nights became as heavy as the long dusty afternoons, and the days at prison were a burden. The chaplain walked slowly home after dark, feeling weighted. He remembered how in May, after the reprieve, he had been as it were blinded by nature and by love. Now it seemed to him that he was—what: angry? Perhaps not that quite; and "blind" after all may have been the case too nearly.

He was more with his family than before. They took their strolls or country excursions, the little girls sedate, charming everyone who saw them, Mrs. Snow straight and slim with her yellow parasol upraised like a flower. It was a straight handsome family. Carpenter remained a few days more and was sent to stay with his mother in his grandmother's house in Elmira, though old Mrs. Snow was not quite recovered. Carpenter had languished and complained all day and slept poorly at night. Snow and his "ladies" waited on the unshaded depot platform to wave him off; the train shook in the heat, rode on tracks that glared through a smoke of heat. They walked some of the few blocks home in the shade of a water wagon to keep cool; where the wagon went the July dust did not make them cough.

Dr. Clark did not visit now, and it was too hot to play lawn games in any case. Snow dragged his chair from the plant porch and sat out half the night staring up into the stars, a pitcher of lemonade beside him in the dark grass. When his wife came to their window at the rear of the house they would look at each other silently.

The pasture on the other side of Snow's fence was crowded with canebrakes in which wild red raspberries hung and were this summer ripe earlier than usual. He and his ladies toiled filling quart buckets all one Saturday morning, which he then took up for a Sunday treat in the prison hospital. He was tired every day, all day, and was constantly stifling yawns; yet he slept badly. He hardly troubled to prepare his sermons, feeling that he knew exactly what he must say; but then he stumbled over them. There was a double sense of time in his life now, which he found disturbing: the slow summer on one hand and Weber's few final days on the other. He lived in both times. He would tuck aside the prickly stems with care, reach in his hand cautiously; he had time; the berries with their ripe close drupelets fell into his palm, each went into the bucket that took forever and amen to fill. The girls were even slower. All were sedate and slow-moving, deliberate, and the level of berries rose in the tin buckets slow as a spring tide, taking forever. But when he carried them up later in the new extension-top carriage, he was suddenly in a dream of haste, driving the little mare too fast for the heat, fearful that every man's salvation depended upon his speed. And then the hours clicked like seconds, swept in a blur of green heat, the horse trailing green foam from her mouth, dust piling in a hot pillar behind. He tugged out his watch every moment; Town Hall's clock seemed to him to clank so often that the air was on fire with time. He woke at night, having dreamed that Weber was dead, that they had killed him secretly at night without telling him, and in a panic he took up his watch from the stand, holding it to the moonlight: jump—tick; and it was morning.

New buildings in town appeared to Snow to sprout in days. The New York Central completed its power house for the electrified cars, which formerly had been run from an old barn. The wooden State Street bridge was pulled down and a stone one thrust into its place: snap! The new brewery went up overnight on Tonawanda Street, and Reverend Shaw's Christ Church was finished and in use in a tick of the clock. South Line Street's sewer was finished; the Burke County Savings Bank put up its new structure—both, it seemed to Snow, in no time whatsoever. Street illumination was in the process of conversion from gas, and already Empire was electrified. It happened so quickly, so ruthlessly, that it made one's head spin. Snow would wander in Clarkville at dawn or after dark, going all the way to the lake's west shore and up into the low hills beyond. In a tick of the clock Weber would be dead. He strolled aimlessly, exhausted, on Division Street at night where the workmen, the poor, and the Negroes lived, awake in the heat: railroadmen, mill hands, brewerymen, laborers, the unemployed lining the walks, filling the saloons. Then night would be gone in an instant of time, quick as thought, and Snow rushed home. Had they killed the man without telling him? In a week Clarkville had been altered, become another town. It was Utica or Rome or a new star: a new world. But then on the Saturday there was that slow morning, the lingering reveille, raspberries falling into his children's small hands, clocks sedate too.

None of this was for God. Snow felt empty. It was all right with the new man Fisch, kneeling in the cage; then he was like a child again, and Fisch was a child. But the times with Weber were without love, and the odd final days were loveless. The red congested summer was no gift for God, no benefaction. This death was no gift.

He tried to tell Weber his fear but could not and in fact knew he should not. He had been wrong about nearly everything. The talks about electricity were all wrong and not for God. Weber turned his back; Fisch, he was sure, would take better to that sort of instruction. And it did no good to admit to Weber that he, Snow, had been a failure; there was no confidence, no pact any longer. Weber turned his back to him.

He rarely prayed except with Fisch. He read books and articles about electricity and the new patents.

He wandered like a peddler everywhere in town and in the blazing country lanes.

From afar he saw Kernahan cycling in company with Taggart, the prison's new electrician. Once he saw Reverend Baird as he had seen him in his dream, sitting alone under a tree, a book in his hands: flannels, straw hat, ordinary collar—everything but the kid gloves. His silken hair floated gloriously about his head; benignantly he read, seated on the bench; sun and shade both beamed upon him; fatherly, spiritually he read in an effulgence of silken glory. Snow strode to meet him, but the closer he got, the smaller grew Reverend Baird until the old man was like a doll one could hold in the palm of one's hand. Then Snow turned away without speaking.

seven

Love or Death
Inside a House

1

". . . on July 11," Dr. Clark read aloud to the summer meeting
of the Burke County Historical Society, of which he was Re-
corder, "Mary Porter Buxton, 49, suddenly after a short illness.
She was the prison warden's wife. She was one of the original
founders, ten years ago, of the Burke County Asylum for Desti-
tute Children and for some years before coming here Secretary
of the Home for the Friendless in Syracuse. Mary was a faithful,
familiar, and well-loved visitor to the convicts in Clarkville State
Prison. A loving wife, a loyal friend, and an exemplary Christian,
she will be sorely missed by all in this community.

"On July 12 Dr. Thomas Wills Willard in his 84th year, my
personal friend and early pilot, Clarkville's oldest practitioner,
eccentric in disposition, charitable and sympathetic . . ."

Fox crossed the street to Central Park, dodging between two carriages, but when he looked back he saw that some of the crowd, which was mostly women, had followed him to the corner of Fifth and Seventy-second, and one raised a fist. It was hot. He sat on a bench for some time watching the nursemaids and babies, and the young men with their young women. It was odd to be idle, however briefly, in the middle of a weekday.

He supposed the reporter had been directed to him by his wife who had no conception . . .

"The *Sun*," the man said.

Fox rose at once and went off along one of the dusty paths, the reporter close.

"The sun is up in the sky. Very hot."

"Did the committee bother you?"

"Not so much as you are doing."

He turned on the newspaperman. "Patients are waiting and patience has fled. What do you want?" In fact he had left his patients, needing air. Yet the pun gave him some pleasure. "*Oh!*" he said when the man did not respond at once. The sky blazed in reflection from roofs of hacks, and their drivers wilted. The crosstown street was all but impossible to negotiate: but Fox, with a long imperious hand upraised, stepped right out; the reporter used him to shield his own passage. "Pull up your horse!" Fox cried. "I am crossing this street!

"I am a physician!"

A driver yelled, "You'll need one!"

Fox relented after a time and addressed the newsman. "The committee in front of my house have confused the matter with their own. The question of whether or not there shall be capital punishment has nothing to do with me or my efforts to secure passage of the electrical execution bill. My purpose was and is to see that men are aided in dealing humanely with those whose lives are forfeit to society under our laws as they exist now." He allowed the man to write. "Weber is fortunate. He will not only have perished without sensation, he will have had carved for himself a little niche in history, having been the first to die by legal decree in this manner.

"No, no. He has not gone crazy. You always hear that sort of thing.

"Yes, I have today received my invitation to witness the execution. No more. I wish you would go and set in the west now since you are the sun; you are uncomfortably hot."

In a better humor he stood across the street from his house and watched. The committee stood silently at the steep brownstone steps before moving in a body slowly toward the park. The woman who had shaken her fist at him carried an illuminated copy of the petition, with which he was already familiar since it had not only come to him in the mail but been published in the *Times*: "Mercy's Appeal to the 'Father of Electrical Execution.'" One of the maids was peeping from behind a second-story curtain. The group started back, talking earnestly among themselves: a lot of unattractive women and raw young men, Fox thought. He had called the police and two patrolmen stood quietly at the curbstone. Fox went back into his house.

3

Clarkville Prison
July 22, 1890

Dr. Henry Hamilton Fox
19 East Seventy-second Street
New York City

DEAR SIR,

I am sorry to trouble you again. Will you volunteer to act as a witness for the people of New York State on August 6th next to the execution of sentence upon Rupert Weber, *alias* Rupert Johnson? If you agree, I will expect you promptly at seven o'clock on the evening of Tuesday August 5th at the main prison entrance, where it will be my pleasure to greet you and the rest of the witnesses. We shall hold a brief meeting in my office upstairs, and then you will be free until early the following morning, at which time you shall report to the prison once more. I do not name the hour here deliberately but will let you know it on Tuesday evening. I have arranged for hacks to meet the afternoon trains at Hartwood and Fort Ann, the east and west stops before Clarkville, for those witnesses who wish to avoid reporters. I have also arranged for you and the others to put up as on the earlier occasion at the Clark House, which remains the only local hostelry I can fairly recommend.

Weber, under the prison chaplain's guidance, has developed an interest in electrical phenomena and machinery. I have not encouraged the study, but Snow is persuaded that it is worthwhile on the theory that ignorance is apt to breed terror in this case; and in the event Weber may prove more docile as a result of what he has learned. I tell you this because your name arose in their conversations, and Weber has several times declared his earnest wish to meet you. Would you be willing to have an interview with the prisoner sometime during the evening of the 5th?

Dr. Nerney writes that you may be agreeable to taking part in the autopsy.

Very truly yours,
HIRAM P. BUXTON

4

19 East 72nd Street
New York City
July 24, 1890

Mr. Hiram P. Buxton, Warden
Clarkville State Prison
Clarkville, New York

DEAR SIR,

I hasten to reply and, with a sense of particular personal duty in this matter, to accept your invitation to perform a sad but necessary office. . . .

I don't disapprove your chaplain's efforts to teach Weber. If he can convince the condemned man of the engine's efficacy, then he shall have done well. I will be pleased to meet Weber and chat with him. Since his wish is "earnest" I feel I am obliged to do so. Perhaps I can do something toward reassuring him, too. I do not want to take part in the autopsy, though I am willing to observe it. If I am asked, I will offer suggestions and comments as it progresses; on this basis I can put my name to the post-mortem report, too, if you like.

Now I must tell you in plain words that I am opposed to the presence in the death chamber of Dr. A. Luft of Buffalo and of his so-called "resuscitator." I have expressed my opposition in a letter to Governor Hill, copies of which have been sent to the other members of the Capital Punishment Commission, and a copy of which I enclose. It is my hope that Governor Hill will forbid the application of any "resuscitator" to Weber after execution and that you will support him if he does. I look forward to seeing you on the evening of August 5th, and meanwhile I remain your respectful servant,

H. H. Fox

5

State of New York
Executive Chamber
Albany, July 22, 1890

Marcus A. Bush, Esquire
Bush, Kelsey, Levy, and Bush
Attorneys at Law
920 Broadway, New York City

DEAR SIR,

Governor Hill has asked me to advise you that the State's titles to all electrical machinery at Clarkville Prison, new, old, and of all manufacturing, are readily shown and that the machines there are lawfully detained. Judicial process in behalf of any manufacturer of electrical machinery to regain any piece of the State's equipment will be vigorously opposed by the State, and the Governor's sympathetic and unofficial advice is that your office does not undertake it.

Very truly yours,
F. T. ROSE
Secretary to the Governor

143

6

The cartoon in the Buffalo *Star-Union* showed figures labeled "Edison" and "Westinghouse" locked in hand-to-hand battle, a chair rigged with wires behind the former, a hangman's rope in the hand of the latter, while through a door marked "Home for Aged Prisoners" "Weber," dragging a bloody ax, is led by a tall, mustached "Buxton" shedding papers marked "G.W. Co. Stock Certificates."

Clark brought it along with him to the Clark House dining room where he met the warden. "If that isn't a libel, I don't know one."

"Never mind," said Buxton.

"Not if you don't."

The room clattered with noise; it was hot; ceiling fans stirred the air. "There is Taggart dining alone. He doesn't have his snickersnee. Shall I ask him to join us? . . . No."

"I may have Stone back," said Buxton, "and divide the work between them."

They smoked cigars in the lobby. A reporter from the *Advertiser*, a young man, hovered.

"Divide responsibility as well."

"Well, perhaps." Buxton paused. "The chaplain is of no help now. He's gone off the deep end with Weber and is feuding with McDade. I particularly need McDade. . . . I'd say Snow was putting himself before his pastoral obligations. Isn't that pride?"

"He isn't proud. Have McDade back."

"I mean to try to before the execution, but Snow won't help."

The reporter kept clearing his throat. He looked at the *Star-Union* open on Clark's knee. "That rag," he said. "They ought to be ashamed."

"What do you want?"

"They told me to ask if you've applied for a stay."

144

"Hill said he won't grant one, so I haven't. I have discovered no cause for a stay thus far and neither has Dr. Clark. You may report that of seventeen invited witnesses sixteen have accepted. I'll wire another four tomorrow; the rest are on the spot. Someone will give you a list when you call at the office. . . . Talk to Dr. Clark, if he's willing. I must get back."

Restlessly, later, Keough silent in his wake, he prowled the prison galleries.

Keough said, "His coffin." They were in the carpentry shop corridor. But P.K. at once saw he might be putting his foot in it; he could not tell what it was safe to say since Mrs. Buxton's passing. A convict's voice came out of the top gallery darkness. "Weber's a kink!" It came trumpeting through the wing, amplified by the steel and quiet. "You're killing a kink, Buxton!" None of the inmates took it up; they did not make a lark of it, which showed the seriousness of their feelings, Keough thought.

He said, "I believe I know who that was," and sent a keeper to chalk the door for punishment in the morning.

7

It was no use. There would be no stay for Weber for a commission. Clark could not see it. In any event, Buxton had tried; and that was the point perhaps, thinking of Mrs. Buxton—that he had tried.

The warden had a dream of Weber lying in his coffin burned black as a Negro by the electricity. Mrs. Buxton wrung her hands, weeping. A dog turned in the center of a road, half crushed, trying to bite its own hindquarters that hurt it.

The warden owned a Navy Colt, which had been modified in the war for cartridges and which he kept in a drawer by his bed. When he woke from the dream he took the pistol out and held it in his hand. He remembered the dog in his dream as the ghost of one he had finished in mercy with this gun years before after it had been run down by a wagon. Now the gun was as comforting as flesh in his palm after the bad dream; and the worn brass in it gleamed beautifully.

He had still the few witnesses to ask. There in the near dark he was visited by a notion of the absurdity of men—that one man waited patient as a dog while others not much different from him after all gathered gravely, one to kill, the others to witness the killing. It was the witnessing that did it, Buxton thought in his bed: assembling to wed lovers, acknowledge a birth, or kill a man, acting in all things before men. The witnessing made it the work of men and God together. He put the gun away, fell asleep, and slept well for the first time since his wife's death.

8

The boat was moored a few hundred yards off his jetty, and Conrad Grace had rowed himself to it. It was his pleasure to be alone with a few feet of line, a couple of rusty spinners tied to its end; never mind high-priced gear and deep-sea fishing; never mind the catch for that matter. His tired unwinding consciousness was central. Around it were the salt air and silence, the club's island clad in spruce, cathedral ribs of rock in the bay, the bay with a texture like twill from the breeze.

He was to remember a voice saying distinctly, "Skin him yourself, sir. It ain't hard."

Grace would skin a deer. The Micmac guide tutored him, and he finally did it, but rather bloodily. At last—pop—the whole thing came free, loose and sliding in his hands like a silk-covered comforter, and still warm. They had gone into all of it, the three-man Commission: the rope, guillotine, the garrote, electricity. Grace had been in favor of morphine first, electricity second; an injection of the drug was beyond doubt merciful and quick, he felt; but Fox opposed it. They could not be sure of the dose, he said; a man might be addicted and resist it; no qualified physician would do the job, and no one else was competent. Grace thought with clarity, placing the words like furniture in a room, that the great reason was that it would give the medical man's medicine a bad name, which was the same as Westinghouse's fear; he fitted out another room with the words "I should not have consented."

When he awoke there were more than a dozen of the eccentric birds, after which he named his schooner, on a nearby island of rock hitching their feet out of the rising tide, wings outspread. When one launched itself into flight they all did with awkward effort. Rowing here and there in Grace's vicinity was a lobster-man, whose name he should know and could not recall, pulling his traps and dropping most again with stolid disgust.

Grace had had a minor stroke; after a moment or two he felt perfectly fine—refreshed in fact, as if he had been asleep instead of unconscious; and he got himself to shore with no trouble at all.

9

"I mustn't miss that."

Grace, his daughter, and his secretary sat on the shingled porch that overlooked the bay and waved punk sticks to keep off gnats. The secretary had brought over the mail including Warden Buxton's invitation.

"Can you tell what I'm spelling?" Grace wove the glowing stick through the darkness. They could not make it out. "A fellow's name." It was his own, in fact.

He gave his family nautical titles: "Second Officer should have caught that." There was a blurring of speech, but only Grace himself was aware of it: ". . . *shoul've caught that.*"

Later the secretary said, "We wonder if you ought not to re-fuse that invitation."

"Why?"

It was not very clear. When his daughter had excused herself and gone in to bed, Grace asked, "Nothing funny going on, is there?"

"Oh, no."

Grace said, "This is not a picnic. No one expects it to be pleasant."

They took breakfast under a striped awning aboard the *Cormorant.*

"*Will* you watch?" asked Miss Grace.

Her father said that witnessing meant watching.

"*Why?*"

"We must see that the sentence of the court is executed as prescribed and so record."

It made her feel ill. She did not finish her breakfast. She did not think that people ought to kill other people at all.

10

The Hartford *Evening Post* reporter and his sketch artist were given the laboratory tour. They heard a violin solo on one of the phonographs, heard their own recorded sheepish voices, and peered into case after dark case of the Wizard's patents. They submitted to the Wheatstone bridge resistance tests that had become a standard entertainment since the Weber hearings. Without enthusiasm, the reporter volunteered to receive shocks of 100 volts of continuous and 100 of alternating; the alternating, he declared, was a great deal less comfortable.

"I want to ask Mr. Edison . . . does he know Stone is asking to be reinstated?"

"I am certain he does not. He knows nothing of Mr. Stone these days." The barnlike laboratories were sweltering.

". . . financial straits; that Morgan favors merger with Thomson-Houston . . ."

"Oh, dear, no."

The sketch artist wandered off to one end of the room and was doing an odd-looking dynamo's portrait. Suddenly, as if by magic, the Wizard himself materialized; he was standing inside the doorway to the stairs, deep-browed, pale-haired in the shadowed loft, his body bent forward to hear, a hand resting on a piece of apparatus, Kennelly at his side, Sulze-Berger behind him. The reporter was silenced, and the artist turned toward the man hungrily.

11

McDade had not been in a saloon since the suspension. He sat rocking on the porch of his house that overlooked the better end of Division Street.

Kernahan stopped by now and then on his way to prison in the evening. He was sorry about the suspension and wanted it clear first off that he wished McDade was back. He did not care for Hearn, who was hard-handed with the cons and stiff with his fellow keepers.

"I'm glad to be out of it."

"You'll miss the pay."

"We have some saved. I'm glad to be out of it." He sat in his undershirt in the fiery heat, the top button of his trousers unfastened, broad feet in a pair of slippers. "I'm old for it." His white rick of hair stood up; mats of gray hair curled over his shoulders and back. He served Kernahan cider and held his own glass in a burly hand, sucking his mustache. Mrs. McDade, who was slim and comfortable-looking, said, "Fred shouldn't be doing that work at his time. He's better home."

Did he want to know how Weber was faring?

McDade said reluctantly, "All right."

But there was nothing out of the ordinary to report. What was clear was that both the lawyers and Buxton had quit trying for a stay, had no doubt been warned off by the Governor.

"What is it—ten days?"

McDade knew perfectly well.

"That night I'll go off the wagon, and when I wake up it will be over."

"Here's what I say," said Mrs. McDade. "I'm against capital punishment."

The tiny house was like an oven. The man and his wife took their meals outside, chatting with neighbors on porches on either hand. McDade would talk about anything except the condemned rooms. Later on, he would sit alone until all hours gazing across Division and the row of houses to the line of chestnuts black at the lakeside and the hills above them. He could name a few of the summer constellations in the south—the only direction he had studied because of the way the porch faced. There was Scorpius dipping like a hook into the horizon, and pale Capricornus higher on his left hand. But the names of things weren't much after all. He would be up early, no matter what time he went to sleep, and pass the morning feeling tired to death. "It was cooler at least in the prison, wasn't it?" his wife asked.

"You must take the smell with that, though."

He was reading now. He liked comic writers in the magazines best, but he read poetry. He read James Russell Lowell and Walt Whitman. "I celebrate myself. . . . And what I assume you shall assume." *I swear I will never again mention love or death inside a house. . . .*

Right. That was right. Men ought both to love and die out of doors as unknowing as animals, without names for themselves or things around them. On Sunday while his wife, always heavy upon this issue, made significant preparations, he tapped his limp-leather Whitman. "I'll attend Mass here. This is my sort of church." But he read the Bible too, though he preferred the Old to the New Testament since he thought it made superior poetry. There was something in all the books of the Bible and nothing in any of them. For the rest, Lowell could not sing like Whitman or

Longfellow—who could?—but he was a poet and had something to say. He loved Whittier and Holmes too and found a place for Riley. Verses in the evening paper would bring tears to his eyes:

> A little brown bird, not many days old,
> Whose home was a nest in the tree,
> With wing folded close, and head on one side,
> Sat thinking, as wise as could be. . . .

The mere notion of verse moved McDade; that a man would write it at all touched him. And a joke was the same. If a man would only begin a joke, he roared with laughter—it didn't matter if the whole joke was funny or not—because he liked the man for his wish to make him laugh, to talk to him, McDade, in this friendly way. It was all the friendly stuff of men, and it was good; anyhow, it could be. Even Kernahan, he thought in his enlarged and sentimental mood, was good.

The night keeper had a new job under Taggart, for which he would be paid on top of the usual bonus: bossing the engine room beneath the dynamo on the 6th of August. He treated it as something to boast about; and McDade thought anyway: "Well, he's a good man despite that."

Major Keough stopped in one evening. He sat on a rocker and, with McDade, watched the trees and hills go dark as jet against the corn-colored sky. He was in his uniform and would not accept even a glass of cider. "Well, they'd like you back," he said to the point.

McDade would need work sooner or later.

"Come back now, then. I'll return Mr. Hearn to his old duties. He's pretty poor potatoes in the death cells in my estimation. . . ."

McDade stopped him.

"All right then, what about Fisch? You'll have to come back, and you'll still have him to do for," said Keough.

But McDade could not bear the thought now; there was no

way of screwing himself up to it, having once quit over Weber, having decided he could look the other way if he chose. He wanted no part now in it.

<h2 style="text-align:center">12</h2>

He had never put it as plainly as Mrs. McDade, to say he was against capital punishment, but that's what it came to in the end. He was against it. He might tell himself that he preferred hanging, but it was pity he preferred before all. Well, it wasn't pity either; it was sense.

Right.

Keough gone, he sat having the silent arguments alone.

Someone, his proposition went, invaded his home—"my castle, if you like"—threatened Mrs. McD. An ex-con perhaps with a grudge; there were always those, though it happened that the ones who had come back on a visit had all been friendly and nostalgic. So your con sneaks in, then. . . . Here it is: years ago with the boys still at home; one of them . . . God forbid, the butcher actually killed one of the boys. Why then in hot blood McDade could go after him (how readily the anger rose imagining it!), tear him into bloody gobs; right! All right. But that was the man in him, doing what was natural to a man in blazing anger under nature's simple jurisdiction. But then society, which was above men because it was all men, was supposed to protect that man from McDade's nature, put him under the law. Then wouldn't you think that all hands could be restrained from killing—when wrath, under the law, had cooled? Would not McDade have restrained himself if his anger had cooled? But then McDade was no longer in it; it was the law then, and you did not, ought not wittingly add a death to a death. If one death was insufficient for any good, if all it brought was despair, then what in the world would two accomplish?

"There it is."

He argued in the night.

Now this: suppose he had done it, killed the man (he pictured a man named Fay in his drama, a brutish ex-quarryman who had been in his charge at Clinton years before after killing his shopmate, a man named . . . a famous case within the prison system), could that be excused? No, though men would praise him for avenging his child. No, sir. Punished or not for it, he was as guilty as Fay had been, guiltier perhaps for having escaped punishment and been praised by men. If right was right, then wrong was wrong whether done out of hunger, greed, or love of God, or passion, or mercy.

He felt Fay, like death, in the house at his back.

All gristle; he had worn an 18 collar, and they could not break his neck, so they had choked him to death on the scaffold.

If Fay had killed one of the boys, he would have killed Fay in hot blood, not cold; but he would have been a guilty man either way.

There it was: men refused their burdens. They went off to church, to the priest: " 'There, there,' the fellow says, the priest: 'You did well (or bad). Here's your ticket: God's forgiveness' "— and so laid their burdens by that they were meant to carry. "Take up all your burdens, says McDade, don't lay one by!" What a swindle: putting it all on God. "What a swindle," McDade said, addressing the hills. If killing was right, it was always so; if it was wrong, it was wrong in every case without exception and not just when it suited a man's book to make it so. Yes, well he would stay right here at home on Sunday morning and take his Mass with Mr. Whitman. Here, let McDade tell you the single difference between Weber and his ax and the State and its electricity: the State had had its chance to cool off and was doing its murder deliberately rather than in hot blood: two deaths where there had been only one before, two divine sparks pinched out instead of one, only the man had leisure to see his death approach.

13

He guessed he knew what the State was up to. Control.

Control over men, over all to benefit a few.

" 'Why, you're not going to let your hardened cases run about loose, are you, Fred?' "

Now be still a moment. It's control they're after in all things large and small, but where you see it is in the prison system. Yes, it's the system's purpose; aren't I telling you? But it's wrong. *I* say it! No books, no trades, no aid in understanding their own natures, nothing of that kind, no: control them; if it were not for the few good wise men in high places the State would control us all, in prison and out. States do that by *their* nature, and they do it with brutality. Never mind the brutal Fay who had been like a hungry beast.

Control.

That's what the cruelty was for: the beatings and executions, the cruel long sentences; for every brutal Fay destroyed went a hundred good men. Never mind. Men are plentiful, and you can always get a ticket, be absolved, find a judge in law or priest in religion to carry your guilt for you. But McDade knew a man must live with his guilt all his life, never give it away; for that was what might keep him from the wrong act another time— the only thing that might. No guarantees . . . He was not in the business of guarantees. But he knew. Yes, they beat them here at Clarkville. He had seen it. Buxton was aware of it and did nothing or was powerless to act since his job offered consent to the State. Here it is: if you beat a man, you weaken him, so that when you stop he is grateful and loves you. You learn to be-lieve in your judges and wardens, to love the screws and scorn the cons. They couldn't hold a prison ten minutes if men knew the authority to beat a man is anyone's for the taking! But they love you for stopping!

"Read 'starve' for 'beat'?"

Now you see it. As simple as that, McDade argued with himself in the sweltering July night. Men love their jailers for not beating them. If you don't welcome the beating—and wasn't the cane a kind of lover's attention when you got down to it?—you love the relief. Yes, stop loving your jailer and you'll be free: not before. You're the jailer? Your authority's right on the ticket: God's laws, the requirements of war, self-defense, the court's general protection; and on the other side: "Guilt absolved, absorbed by the community of men!" Why not surrender the ticket and be free too?

Control:

One criminal beating another and earning love for it when he stopped, the rats ruling the mice. They have the mice by the ears.

"What are you then—an anarchist?" asked the imagined inquirer.

Very well, he supposed he was: call him an anarchist then.

If it was wrong for men to kill men, then it was wrong in every case without exception *ad finem*, and a whole globeful of judges could not make it right even one time. And he was an anarchist. What a swindle when men call wrong right and then call that justice! What a swindle. And it was cowardice to put your burdens onto others, whether McDade was an anarchist or not. "*I* say it!" There it was.

14

Buxton came personally to the house to ask McDade to return. One evening the chaplain came and sat on a rocker on the little porch; he gave Division Street an engaging look.

"I'm sorry I lost my temper, Sergeant."

All right. But he would not return. He could not.

eight

Weber Delivered

1

He woke up causing a commotion. Kernahan was there in his cage handling him, slapping up and down his legs with the billy. He guessed he had screamed. As if he meant to be sure, he did it again: that was it, for the remnants of the earlier shouts lingered like smoke throughout the chamber and were disturbed by the new one. Kernahan was whispering fiercely into his ear, "Too late for that! You had your chance on trying that."

His arm stood up hard. Images of Jenny had ridden him half the night.

2

Weber had plenty to keep him occupied. He was busy, and he went briskly about his business. He had a few thoughts by this time, and he kept looking over the hand of cards he had to play. They were not bad, taken altogether.

Kernahan had called the night physician, a man Weber did not like, and the doctor came promptly. "Well, now what's all this? Are you having nightmares?" He was not permitted to give the condemned man anything to help him sleep. He hung about outside of the cage uneasily; Weber wished it were Clark there. He liked Clark.

"He thinks to get his review at this late date," said Kernahan, "but he knows it's out of the question."

It was no card for him. He ignored it.

Kernahan off. Hearn on. Weber did not waste any time with these matters.

"What are you: Irish?"

He did not much like Hearn.

When the keeper gave his arrogant little nod, Weber said, "Germans are better." He was brisk and talkative; his own thoughts—the hand of cards he had to use to give him help—ran always under any dialogue like a stream against a bank. "The Irish ain't much. I know them. They keep to themselves, don't they? And they're into everything—the politics—like monkeys. Scratch each other like monkeys. They're worse than Jews."

Hearn could not bear a great deal of teasing. "Bugger yourself," he said in his strangled voice.

"Show me how."

He was quick now.

He looked into the hard self-satisfied face of the screw with its woman's peak of blue-black hair growing low into the forehead, curling back without a part like a black washboard. Weber missed McDade and said so.

"Yes, he's a fine German, ain't he?" replied Hearn, stung.

He searched the guard's face. He was quick.

"Is it time yet?"

"What?"

To bugger himself. He gasped with laughter.

He glanced at the top one of his cards: the Wizard. It was the high one. The course of his good thoughts never ceased. His hard arm was a card.

"Good morning, Fisch," he called briskly. Or at lights-out: "Good night, Fisch. How does it feel to be a fish?"

The other was a fish out of water, a poor fish.

"Are you a pike or what?"

"I ain't anything of that sort."

"Are you a flounder?"

The other condemned man rarely spoke. Weber had to prod and poke to get a syllable out of him.

"Well, you're a puffer then." Silence from behind the mat. Silence from the keepers' cubicle from Hearn or Kernahan—waiting for Weber to get rid of it. "Well, p'r'aps not." And he would start again, naming the fish he knew.

"How do *you* like to be tormented on your name?" Fisch would plead at last.

"Go on. Try it on Weber."

But you could do nothing with Weber; and in any case the other man had no heart for joking.

"Why are you in a sweat? Don't you have the appeal yet?" He put it to the screw: "Don't he? And appeals beyond that? Why is he sweating?" Fisch was supposed to have shot a fellow with a pistol in a saloon in New York City. Seeing the man, it was not possible. Weber, quick now, set himself to think it over and concluded that Fisch had not done it.

"You want your lawyer to hire a detective to get more evidence."

"I did it all right," came the voice muffled from the other side of the mat.

Never mind: it was not possible.

He could look in at the other man during his exercise. Despairing, Fisch sat curled like a child on his bunk in a cage that was a counterpart of Weber's except for the banjo in the corner and the evangelical books and pamphlets scattered across his table, and the man himself. Weber gazed at him in silence, considering. It made him angry. "Can't you look at me?" And at last he would turn away without having satisfied himself, considering. Why, it wasn't possible.

To hell with it.

At night he pretended to be having a nightmare and screamed. Kernahan came out hissing. Fisch started awake, crying, "Wait!" Weber felt himself sink. The cards were no good, no use to him. The bit he had learned from Snow before Snow had turned from him . . . what good was it?

Later he lay broad awake squinting out at the frozen stars. He shivered and shivered in the old way, a whipped child, and rose near dawn to pull on more clothes. His arm had failed him in the old way. He had, he discovered, wet his bedclothes a bit. It set him back.

3

Yet he could think it over, couldn't he?

That was the job for him. Wasn't it something after all: Weber dark, remote in his cage at dawn, coiled into himself like a foxy man, putting two and two together? Thinking! Snow had brought in a photograph of the Wizard seated in his laboratory, white-blond hair falling in a sweep across his forehead, black Lincoln tie around the wing collar, snowy shirtfront, black coat and shiny black waistcoat; on the table before him in the photograph was an incandescent light vase half as big as his head with the miniature scaffolding of wires inside it and a brass knob at its bottom. Snow said he could not leave the picture with him. Never mind. Weber saw it anyhow clear as day in his mind, and he worked on it. By midmorning he was right again. He had done a bit of thinking. His arm came up handsomely. Aces back to back, his arm now and the Wizard. Jenny, face up, was about mid-range in the hand: the knave of hearts.

Briskly:

"Are you a sucker fish?"

The man complained to Keeper Hearn, who told Weber to be silent.

"I was asking. I am curious."

With the cornet and harmonicas going at lights-out, Weber shouted, "Fisch, let's hear a tune on that! Can't you play it?"

Hearn said, "He don't want you to talk to him, Weber."

> Indeed the kisses are my own,
> Their number I've forgot;
> The smiles a long time since have flown,
> They're yours, I want them not!

. . . sang the invisible tenor.

Hearn, gay for him, made noisy kissing sounds; but Weber, with narrowed eyes, considered. He tucked that away: ". . . the kisses are my own" to use later in the dark, perhaps with Jenny. He had now to take deep breaths to calm himself. From one of the blocks nearby a violin scraped out the hymn Snow had taught him long ago, a year ago. There was no notion of that setting him back, was there?

"What is it you have: a banjo? Why the hell don't you play it?"

Here he went again. To hell with it. And anger at himself sprang up in him. He could not manage at this rate. The tenor sang with the violin:

> Hold Thou Thy Cross before my closing eyes. . . .

Shit.

Presently there was the tapping out of prisoners' messages to each other, ticking up and down the drains, muted here like crickets' singing. He did not know the codes anyhow; he was the condemned man, not an old con. The life of the prison evening sank achingly deep into him as if he were water, so that he needed deep breaths to keep right. Wasn't it all shit? Surely it could not go. The image of Edison grew faint in his mind's eye. The clever animal in him slept. But the kisses in the other song brought Jenny, Jenny brought back the Wizard, and at length Weber lay alive once more and wise. He could trust himself for the moment not to be so angry, not to fear, to drown in fear, and not to be "set back." He felt confidence that the bit he had built might keep and that he could manage. He could manage, he supposed. He slept, woke with a shock, dozed again. In the morning he came right around the track to anger.

4

The chaplain glanced in, tormented-looking. It was as if a dark net had been cast across his face.

"Go on. What do you want? It's all the poor fish, ain't it?" He jerked his head at the mat angrily. "Don't trouble about me."

Go on! Weren't they two of a kind?

But he had to listen to their murmur from the other cage. When, later, Snow exercised his privilege, had the guard open Weber's cage, and entered uninvited, the condemned man sat squarely with his back to him, legs flung one over the other in an arrogant manner. Snow asked, "May I stay for a moment?"

Weber shrugged.

"I've brought in our book."

"I don't want to hear it," he said briskly. "I don't care. It don't interest me."

"Am I to take it that nothing I say will interest you?"

He shrugged. Why should he give the little cock the least bit of satisfaction? If he held a few cards, they were his, even if Snow had helped him to one or two with his "lessons." He wanted them, not Snow, and the chaplain had turned away.

"Brother, may I pray to God here?"

He flung a word over his shoulder to Snow. He was insolent.

When, instead of leaving, the chaplain sat mute beside him on the bunk and Weber felt the hard little thigh next to his own, it gave him a cramp of horror and disgust. But when he went at last: "That's right," he thought bitterly, "turn away from me."

5

By now it was clear enough that Mrs. Buxton was dead. She had used to come at around eleven every morning she was well, the sun reaching his window on her arrival, departing strictly with her. He missed her.

He filled one of the remaining days watching the weather: a clear, fiery late July morning and noon; toward dusk clouds piled up like surf, grayish-green and threatening, but it did not rain. Such heat did no one any good, and rain would help the poor farmers. Heat reached even into this basement chamber. During the hot night he thought of Jenny, in the morning of the woman: gray and sick. And he deliberately confused them, having Mrs. Buxton raise his arm for him. It was the sort of image he denied himself at earlier times; but now he denied himself nothing. Often in the morning he glanced up half expecting to catch Mrs. Buxton there looking in at him. At almost the same moment, twenty-four hours later, that he had started his consideration of the weather he stopped.

6

He had the hole card, an ace, another ace up. He had a red jack. That was another knave drifting down like a leaf. He needed . . .

7

Principal keeper was always making a party of it. He took the view that an entire man made the effort to be cheerful in adversity. He would open the cages and have them out into the common area beneath the window.

"You boys should get to know each other. Here you are, you know: you ought to be friends."

Weber didn't think much of the fish at Keough's party today, so he gave him a hard look, which made the other droop against the wall. Despair seemed to have pulled the insides out of him: a little dust bag of a man, trembling with terror, flung miserably up against the wall. Keough looked him over with distaste too. The sight of Fisch made nothing easier. The little New Yorker turned from them, groaning; it was as if he were under water, muddy-yellow; his visage darted and twisted out of sight: a regular fish.

"Why *not* play that musical instrument?" Keough would ask at last. "I and Weber want cheering up."

No use. There was the dollar scrap of baldness displayed on the top of Fisch's bent head, which anyhow would one day save the barber some work. He spoiled the party always. Keough would sigh dramatically. Little and dry as he was, patches of sweat soaked through his uniform under the arms and across the small of his back.

He locked them up again, this party over. Chaplain Snow came along, had a word with the principal keeper, and went into the other cage without a glance at Weber. And in a moment Weber could hear them going on like a sad pair of doves gurgling.

All right.

8

He turned his supper away.

Near dusk he began to shiver, though it was hot.

Then, seeing Hearn's big sheep's head poking about—why, that was more than enough for Weber. That served.

"Here! You Irish cunt! Ain't you ugly?"

He screamed.

He screamed again. He flung back his head and crowed like a rooster.

Hearn brought his gun to bear. "Shut up!" As if a tap had been turned, sweat sprang out all over his face. "What's wrong with you?" It had been Kernahan's watch the other times; he was frightened.

Fisch had leaped to the door of his cage. "What's wrong?"

Weber screamed.

Hearn was shouting for help.

Weber bayed and crowed, throwing back his head.

A pair of screws stumbled down the iron staircase and ran through the condemned rooms to Hearn. "Shut up!" Hearn kept shouting back at Weber. Weber could see that the bastard's eyes were rolling with fright. All three guards were white as paper. That's right. There was no other ease than this for him just now. He tried them out as he would soon be tried. The day watch shoved his shotgun into the hands of one of the pale screws and tore his keys from his belt. "Stop it now, Weber!" he cried. "You're disorderly!"

Weber dropped to his knees, wide awake. It was as if he had been sleeping for years. Yes, and his arm was up stiff too. He flung himself about on the floor of the cage. Hearn had come in to him. He felt the man's hand on him and at once exploded into his trousers.

The spasm calmed him down.

9

"Can't you give me something? I'm tired waiting by now." He wanted something to kill him.

"Oh, dear." Three things against that: the law of the land, the religious moral law, and the power of the oath (an oath was in the nature of a bargain with God; a promise, really) he had sworn when he became a medical man to help preserve life and never, never to take it. Clark said, dismissing it, "Now we will just listen to you tick, Rupert."

He liked Clark.

He lay obedient on his bunk while the doctor, seated on the three-legged stool and hunched over his watch, held one of Weber's wrists pinched between a thumb and two long fingers. His legs were crossed; his bag, rust-red with wear at the creases, stood open at his feet. Nickel gleamed on the stethoscope; throat sticks bound in a bundle and other gadgets lay in their plush nests inside the bag; there were purple and green bottles, tins, and syringes; next to the bag Clark's boot buttons glistened: man and all seemed fixed, permanent in the gloaming of the cage. . . . Clark was tall. He had silver hair, neither thick nor thin, which lifted in gentle cresting waves on either side of a center parting. His eyes were gray with deep lines around them; he wore pince-nez, the glass of which reflected pink in the dying light. Weber saw some short ice-gray hairs in the nostrils of his nose; his hands, one of which held Weber's wrist, were big as a plow-swain's, yet cool, and scrubbed marble-white, with a few toast-colored spots over the backs of them; his lips were hard now with counting.

"Who took you the oath?"

"That was when I received my degree from school."

There it was. An oath. Weber had missed out on all that. No one had ever asked him to swear one until the court. It might have been better if they had.

At a venture, trying the man: "She was always on at me because I didn't get my arm up for her, not more than twice in the six months we lived on South Pearl, maybe half a dozen times since we come to Buffalo. Here you are: I was busy on the wagon, getting in with the commission men, setting up the route. I thought: when I am settled down and get rid of my business worries the arm will come up all right. It did later, but you might say all my business worries were over by then, since I was before the court." He added, as if indifferent, "It's right now."

Clark was not sure he understood.

"My cock."

He saw that he must explain, which made him cold. "It's what we really fought about. It's the truth of why I licked her and why I'm here."

Clark turned away the blind pink discs of glass that covered his eyes. Weber thought he would say something about what he had told him, but instead he asked, "Do you know what the date is, Rupert?"

"The 29th."

"It is July 30th." He wanted to know the charge against Weber, the date of the trial, the name of his first lawyer, the reason for and the date of his reprieve in the spring.

Weber sat up. "I ain't crazy."

"I don't really suppose you are. Why did you make that fuss for Corporal Hearn?"

It was because Snow and Fisch got on his nerves, but he lied: "I was pretending, to get a committee on me. Now I'm sorry I did."

"Why?"

"Because I ought to be what I really am."

When he could see the gray eyes again, he thought: "He don't like me."

It made him cold. "What is your name?" he asked, cold.

"Stephen."

"All right, Stephen," Weber said.

Clark packed up his bag and snapped it shut. He said, "You will do very well, you know, Rupert, because this machine is a perfect wonder and you are a calm fellow and very brave. But you must leave it all in our hands and not interfere; leave it to us. It is on us now, and we accept our responsibility. I accept mine.

Now: do you accept yours without any reservations, and leave it all to us."

The doctor was as cold as winter. Weber thought bitterly: "All right, Stephen."

10

He woke after midnight and saw a pair of dogs in the cage. One sat back powerfully on its legs, hindquarters a bit raised, alert; he looked this way and that; then big jaws parted to show teeth like silver coins. The other one was sniffing up and down the bottom edge of the cage wall, its head lowered between its powerful shoulders, backside up, tail stiff. Hunting dogs.

Weber did not move.

In the morning he said:

"Did you see our visitors, Kernahan? There were two dogs in here last night."

"I guess you dreamed them."

Yes. Weber was quick: "Say, anything you find in that bucket is yours, Kernahan."

Keeper Hearn came on.

Weber yelled, "Cockadoodle-doo!"

He gasped with laughter. "How did you like that fit, Hearn? You were scared, weren't you?"

"You're the one was wet."

"That's all right. I'm a man, anyhow." Weber was not ashamed of that. Unaccountably, he felt fine. He remembered the farm again, how that storm built from nothing, from a stirring of new leaves, from dryness and light into death. Feeling as if he were on the farm, he said to Hearn, "That put you in a sweat, didn't it? You wanted to blow my head off. I saw your face. Does Keough know you had to yell for help? Ain't this your job to take care of Weber? It makes me laugh."

"Something you said . . . If you wasn't in there, a prisoner, I'd kill you for it."

"Yes, well, won't you?"

"You said 'Irish,' and you used a certain word for a certain part of a woman."

"Well, ain't you Irish?"

He gasped and gasped. The keeper's face went scarlet. He nodded. "All right." He kept nodding.

"You'll kill me for this, won't you?" said Weber gasping.

"Well, I'll part your hair with this billy, and you won't like that."

Weber did not mind. "Come on in."

"What are you: a Molly?—what you did."

It made Weber laugh. "No, I'm a man, which is more than you are." He was not ashamed. Shame was old ways hanging on. He admitted everything to himself, denied nothing. If you denied something at the end, well, what was the point? Weber was not going to lie to himself if he could help it. "Cockadoodle-doo!" And Hearn was a bastard.

Well, he had explained to Clark about Jenny and him.

He threw his head back, crowed like a rooster. Hearn got that worried look again, his flat cat's brow wrinkling. Invisible in the cage nearby, Fisch cried out, "What is it?" nervously. The keeper was fingering the shotgun, seldom out of his hands, and glancing toward the stairs.

"Let me out for exercise!"

"No, indeed, prisoner!"

"You're in a sweat, ain't you?"

Weber told him to his face. Hearn was an Irish so-and-so.

When principal keeper came down with tobacco, which he allowed in any amount now, he put a stop to the noise, but Weber did not miss the hard look he gave Hearn. P.K. moved to Fisch's cage and threw him a loud good morning. Weber had the advantage over them all, knee-deep in foaming brown water with Father and his brother. The old man had picked up a drowned hen and was looking at it bitterly, and the fowl's dull pebble eye stared back: I'm dead—death in the milk-blue eye. Keough said, "Cheer up, Jack," to Fisch. "The sun hasn't fallen out of the sky, has it? Have a look, Hearn. Is it up there yet?" Weber smoked one cigarette after another until the keeper, who blamed his reproof on the convict, went around sniffing. "Mustn't I smoke in your parlor, Hearn?"

He took a walk outside his cage later, quieter, and had a look at the other condemned man. Too bad. Fisch sat curled like a child on his bunk, bony and small-handed, face hidden, and tufts of dusty hair stuck up around his bald spot; he looked like some dusty sack brought up out of a cellar. Weber stared.

It was too bad.

From the vantage of the farm he grew sober and sad. Someone —who?—had once looked at him too as if he were no more than a sad little bag of dusty humanity, like this Fisch: with pity. That was not his father he knew. Then who?—briskly, thinking it out. But no answer ever came. It made him sober, feeling pity for this child-man, Fisch, and he shook it off.

Later, with Hearn back in his cubicle, he looked out and . . . there was Mrs. Buxton!

"You like Dr. Clark now," she said. It made her the least bit jealous.

"I told him too much," he said, his mood failing, remembering the coldness.

She hung limply about in front of the cage in her long-sleeved flowered gown and straw bonnet, carrying her book.

"I won't thwart the Wizard anyhow," he said.

"Better not."

Hearn looked out of his little room at Weber.

"It's an oath," Weber said.

"Are you addressing me?" Hearn asked.

Chaplain Snow came down the iron stairs.

11

Creeping Jesus.

"Go and see Fisch. I don't want you."

"I came to see you."

Weber was silent.

After what seemed a long time the chaplain said, "I've failed you in every way, have I not?"

Jesus H. Particular Christ!

Weber stared at the handsome man.

12

The warden arrived for his call while Snow was still in with Weber. He had received Clark's report on Weber's recent behavior and passed it on to the proper office. "I don't advise you to be hopeful."

"I ain't hopeful on it."

Buxton did not meet the other's gaze. "Dr. Fox writes me that he will be pleased to meet you."

Pleased! All right.

The warden and Snow went off together, but Snow came dragging back later, pale and drawn fine. Weber studied him. "Here you are," he said. "Bring me the Bible back, if you like."

The third ace.

Snow's eyes shone. "Well, Rupert!" he kept saying.

13

Thomas Alva Edison had been born in Milan, Ohio, during a heavy snowstorm, morning of Feb. 11, '47: "Al" to everyone from the first. His head was too large for his body; he didn't play like other children; at fourteen he was already a young capitalist with two stores under his management; he published his own paper and was candy butcher and newsboy on the local trains; he learned telegraphy and as a sixteen-year-old operator came up with the first invention: a gadget to let his machine check into Central at required intervals while the Wizard himself caught up with his sleep. . . .

14

There was the Bible over on the table as of old, with the slate and chalk next to it. He got off the bunk and, in the light of the gas jet that went all night outside of the cages, had a look.

Fisch said, "Come over to me, come over to me," in his sleep.

"Come over to me, Kernahan," Weber called. He was wide awake, quick. He had turned the heavy boards of the Bible, let it fall open on its spine, and put a finger at random on a verse. Kernahan stood scowling and uneasy; like Buxton now, he would not meet the condemned man's eyes.

"What does this say?"

"Dead?" cried Fisch in his sleep.

Weber held the book to the mesh of the cage, and Kernahan reluctantly put on his glasses. " 'Hear now this, O foolish people, and without understanding; which have eyes and see not; which have ears and hear not: Fear ye not me? . . .' "

The night watch would read no more. He would not look at Weber. It was enough in any case. "Which have eyes . . . which have ears . . ." He pored over the book, the familiar illustrations. Solomon in all his glory, the Queen of Sheba.

Weber tore the polished page with the picture on it from the book. "Which have eyes . . ."

"Don't. You are wrong to do that, Weber." He was, for Kernahan, mild and subdued. He did not look into the other's face.

171

"P'r'aps I need it for the bucket."

Here was one he remembered of a woman in a rough gown, a sheet across her head: "The Other Mary," it was named. He pulled it right out of the book. Kernahan turned his back on him, the gesture saying, I am through with you.

No loss.

Good night.

He took Solomon, Sheba, and Mary to bed with him, though it was near dawn, put them face to face under the covers against his hard arm. Which have ears . . . He tried to picture Fox, father of electrical execution, but came out instead with the solemn and kindly Wizard white as an egg in his dark old laboratory.

He dozed. When he did not wake himself with the little dream-shock, the bugs would wake him. Fisch carried on like an infant in the other cage, and Weber had to fling the pity far from him: the one bad apple that could ruin the bushel. Briskly, he thought: "What about Jenny?"

She come in and caught him in the poolroom at back getting full with Billy. She stamped the snow off her old shoes. She was so cold and wet and the room so hot from the stove that when she threw her shawl back steam rose from her hair; she pulled off her wet wool gloves and steam rose from her hands, which were red as beets and puffed with cold. The two started to laugh at her and could not stop. Pretty well intoxicated: a pair of rum-dones. Oh, my! Phil for Philadelphia was his nickname around the commission houses; they were Phil and Bill, a team, close hard buyers both of them, who never left off pushing the wagon through the bitter Buffalo streets until the last sack of onions or whatever it was was sold, then they went and drank a few. There was $300 in the trunk in his house; he told the officer to bring that, trunk and all for safety, to the station. "Officer," he said on the way, "I'm hungry. Let me stop for a nickel's worth of fried cakes"—their name for doughnuts in Buffalo. And he did. His first lawyer tried to make out they gave him brandy at the precinct station to get him drunk to confess. But that was not it. He come down carrying the child Ella in his arms, the four-year-old still asleep, put her down at the landlady's door. "I killed her mamma," he declared. "You don't mean it!" she said. And: "I opened the door, saw a person lying there on hands and knees," Mrs. Kane said in court, "rather her knees and arms, swaying backwards and forwards, with blood all over her head and hair and down on the floor. I turned and saw him . . ." "Hold up your head, please, Weber. That man?" said the judge. "Yes, that one. I said, 'This is brutal, man. Call a doctor.' He was wiping his hands then. He turned and went out, and I thought he was going for the doctor, but he brought his friend to see, and then they went out together." . . . Swore in Charles M. Smith, M.D., for the People: "Well, a young woman, about thirty, identified to me as Jenny Johnson, was brought into the Fitch Accident Hospital at around ten A.M. March 29th, this year. . . . A plain dress, a working dress . . . She was about 130 pounds, five feet six inches in height, dark complexion. When chloroform was administered and the hair shaved, twenty-six wounds through the scalp were revealed and evidence of fracture beneath the scalp. . . . A three-by-two fracture . . . Why, by that it is meant that when the pieces were removed a cavity of that extent was revealed. That's right, those are the pieces in that box. Yes, I judge that they are normal as to thickness. . . .

"Some discoloration of the throat and breast.

"She died at 12:50 A.M. on March 31st, about forty-two hours after the attack on her.

"Following post-mortem examination, the body was buried by Crowley Brothers."

He woke once more and there were the dogs. They sat attentively. When they turned their heads there was a rattle, a little clattering. Were they clockwork animals like some Weber had seen at the department store one Christmas? They rose whirring,

173

came a step nearer the bunk, and sat back once more, attentive; it was as if they were waiting to be fed.

He dozed and woke; one had advanced to the bunk and laid its heavy head down—right there close to Weber's face.

He liked dogs all right but horses better. A horse would answer to your hands on him better, and a horse did work like a man where a dog only lay around eating and using up breathing space to go on a hunt now and then. Nevertheless, Weber took a hand from between his thighs and thrust it out of the blanket. The animal's eyes followed it. That was a heavy head, like iron; it was like a weight of iron shoving the bunk down. The reddish eyes followed the con's hand. Why didn't it turn and bite him? The other sat back looking around with that noise, as if the one had been told off to set a watch, and the other . . .

Its breath was as hot as the sun. Weber had burst into a sweat and it soaked him through. What was that? He had forgotten Solomon and The Other Mary in the nest there with him; they had crackled, startling him. The dog's breath, not a dozen inches from his face, was fire.

Weber's hand hovered, then rested on the blazing head.

15

"Forget it. You done your best to keep from killing me with the dynamo, and you lose out, that's all. You tell Westinghouse I said you done your best on the legal end.

"I learned a little in here and can put together two and two. Edison is a businessman, a capitalist. That's *what he is* and was at fourteen I am told, and what is he now? Forty-three and a millionaire. So give him credit for it. Yes, you agree: in a pig's bung. And I say he is interested in the public first and the public safety.

"I am telling you, ain't I? What do they call you? All right, Marcus, you can be sure since I am telling you. 'I don't care for a fortune as I do for getting ahead of the other fellow,' is what he said. Safety first, then getting ahead in the race, then the money. Shouldn't he get his money? But your man—that's *all* he cares about, and safety last.

"Never mind, Marcus. That's all. It don't do. I don't ask you to come up on the hot train, and I don't ask you to go back. You're a free man. It's up to you."

16

He enjoyed sitting back easy on his bunk now and just gazing at Snow, who had been like a child about Weber taking the book, and came in and sat with him as pleased as Punch, smiling. But the cage seemed smaller with the other man in it and crowded with something besides two men. Did Snow feel it too?

When the chaplain had his square chin up, blue eyes squinting and fixed on the cage wall, that was his silent prayer for Weber. Let him pray. Maybe he could go back to it for Snow—really, instead of pretending. It beat out Fisch for certain, because Weber was first; Fisch would have him afterward. He lay back on the bunk gazing and gazing at the fair little fellow who was no older than he was—a bit younger, he supposed. He tried to picture Snow as an old man, imagining he had got commuted and could know him, but that was no good.

There was something this cage was heavy with when the other was in it, and it was not like with Clark. He had loved Clark for what: a few minutes in all?—and then finally had himself said too much and altered it for both of them; it was what could happen between two people, apparently, though he had never noticed such things before. Now, you take this fair little fellow who admitted he had failed: let him pray, Weber said. Hadn't he earned the right? Weber would not stop him; and who could tell? Perhaps he would go back to it after all.

Mrs. Buxton came later and stood drooping outside of the cage.

"Well, now I'm back with Snow," he told her, not wishing to be more definite than that.

She said she was delighted, yet her voice was sad: "Listen to what he tells you. P'r'aps you'll learn something to your benefit."

"I don't say how far I'll go with him."

> My heart leaps up when I behold
> A rainbow in the sky:
> So was it when my life began;
> So is it now I am a man;
> So be it when I shall grow old,
> Or let me die!

She recited poetry.

He let the old habits go and admitted anything. Nothing was denied. What was Mrs. Buxton at the time of her death—fifty?—and with disease eating her. Yet at night he used the thought of her under her clothes as he used Jenny, and it was all right. *It was all right.* He had the clothes off her entirely in the cage, examined her without fear, his hands everywhere, put her on the bunk, and went to work with his arm. Now that was a different thing from these renewed visits of hers. It was only when she was gone that he took her as he took Jenny. The visits, when she read out of the book or said a few words, were proper.

"Do you never think about your wife—your true wife?"

She meant who he had left to go with Jenny.

It turned out to be a good card.

He had taken the old bitch to Atlantic City for the honeymoon, and after a bathe they came back to the room. She had all her clothes off except the bathing stockings and sat on what they call the hassock, turned away from him. First she pointed one foot out, rolled down the stocking, and let it drop off onto the floor; she did the same with the other. Then she unwound her long black plait of hair and divided it up into loose ropes, then toweled each rope dry, bending forward and pulling it over her face. She dried it forever. She would take all day. Now she had had a husband before him—long ago—and that one had given her a gold toothpick, which she prized, so now she dried her hair and chewed on the toothpick, turned away from him, until at last it was all dry and lay in a broad fan across her dark smooth hard-muscled back, and she sat forward like a man, an elbow on each knee, breathing hard from the exercise, the bubs hanging down between her knees. In the dawn he went to the beach alone. The sand was cold, though the air was warm. It started to rain, and the rain made dimples on the water and touched him as gently as a mother.

That was silent.

The summer of '81. A card to play.

He liked slouching back and watching Snow at his silent prayer; he kept his lips hooked up into a rusty smile. He could see it disturbed the little chaplain, disturbed and excited him.

He had to be careful; this was not for pennies or nickels.

He smoothed out King Solomon and The Other Mary and stuck them back into the book. If Snow had noticed their absence or their condition now, he said nothing.

"One thing: I never acted out I was a kink."

That was very much to his credit.

Yet he had to go carefully here: there were those who would say that if he was not pretending then he might be crazy in fact. "Here you are: I lose my nerve and pretend, then I'm all right again and I can tell them I am. But I'm right all the way through." He did not want a stay.

"But you have your nerve now?" asked Snow with certainty, with triumph.

"Yes!"

They turned to look at each other, Snow by the table, his neat hand on the book, Weber slouched on the bunk smiling a little. It was exciting, better than liquor; the cage was heavy with what now lay between the two, the possibility.

Their blue eyes were just the same shade.

"I am *glad* you took the Bible back, Rupert."

Weber glanced from the book to the man, considering. He kept glancing over the hands of cards he saw in his mind as well.

"I feel the air is cleared. Now when I pray here, my words fly straight up unimpeded. Don't you feel God is near us at this moment? I sense Him here in this place. If I look quickly enough, I think, willingly enough, over there . . .

"Of course, everywhere . . ."

He said, "Rupert, we are very close to the same thing. It doesn't matter what you call it; it's the same."

Careful.

He lay back and gazed at him.

The Wizard looked on in his mind.

Snow asked, "Will you get onto your knees with me now?"

Jenny looked on and Mrs. Buxton, and now the old bitch with them, rolling down her stockings. The Wizard was there, watching in a friendly way. Weber leaned back and made the chaplain's blue eyes meet his. Careful. "Later p'r'aps."

17

The new electrician, Taggart, came down. He looked into the chamber where Weber and Fisch were caged, then turned into the short corridor that led to the death room. Weber heard him moving about in the chamber where he knew the chair was and, after a moment, in the switchboard room. The dynamo was started up with a great rumbling noise at the other end of the prison, and in a moment Weber heard what he now understood to be the closing of the main circuit switch; there was the smell of scorch.

Fisch was saying, "What is it?" excitedly, over and over.

"The executioner."

Weber heard Fisch begin to throw himself about in his cage.

Hearn went over to him. "You're all right," he said in his stiff way. "What's the matter, Jack?"

The man uttered some sound.

"He's making sure it works, Fisch," called Weber. "You want that, don't you?"

"Pipe down," said Hearn.

"It is all scientific now," Weber said seriously.

Taggart came into the chamber, spoke a word to Hearn, then bustled across to Weber, chewing his mustache. He was a dark stocky man dressed elegantly in the height of fashion—or so Weber supposed—and he spoke with an odd sort of English accent. "I am the electrician," he said. "We have not met before."

"Taggart's your name."

"That's right. I want to mention one or two things, so listen with attention, and then there can be no mistake. The point of this procedure is lost unless we move quickly when the time arrives. You will be prepared in this cell by the barber to assure a good contact with the head electrode. When the door here is opened, either by Warden Buxton or the principal keeper, you will step out quickly, going before all the others who have been in with you except the warden; accompany him down that passage and proceed to the end of it, to the largest room. Is that clear so far?"

Weber nodded. He knew Fisch was listening too.

"You will pass the keepers' room and then the switchboard room. The final one has the chair in it. The witnesses will be there, their presence required by law, seated in two rows of chairs facing the chair in which you will sit. I imagine that Mr. Buxton will make a general introduction, to which you may respond but need not. There will be more than twenty people, and it will look like quite a crowd to you; never mind that. After you speak, if you do, go to the chair at once and sit in it. You cannot mistake the chair, though you have not seen it. It is large and heavily constructed; it is bolted to the floor. You will see the headpiece and the wires. There are straps for your head and body and others for your limbs. Mr. Buxton will adjust all of the straps—there are eleven of them—as rapidly as possible. Since you will no doubt be perspiring, he will towel your head dry where it has been shaved and then adjust an electrode to the spot; he will adjust another to the base of your spine where your clothing will have been cut for the purpose. Then he will step back so that he is visible to me at the switchboard, and give me a signal, and I will close the circuit. Is that clear?"

Yes. "I understand that." Snow had given him all that.

"You sit at once; no delay, understand? If the new method is to serve, speed is of the first importance. I should say promptness, because I don't mean that you are to run as if it were a race. Simply step along smartly beside the warden, neither before nor behind him. A keeper will be behind you, and there may be another in front. Once more: introduction, which you acknowledge if you like; sit down; two straps to the head, one to the body, two to each limb; two electrodes: head and spine; Buxton steps back; signal; switch closed. If I were allowed, I would run a rehearsal and take you to see the chair and sit in it, but Buxton will not permit it. Your best plan in any event is to obey at once and without thought any order you are given.

"What is it?"

He stood impatiently, chewing on the big mustache.

"Is that dynamo right?"

"It is in perfect order. It generates up to two thousand volts. There is no problem there at all. If I may say so, there are no problems anywhere."

"Will it mutilate me?"

"It will not, my word."

Yes, Snow had said the same.

When the electrician had gone, he heard the terror in Fisch's silence and pitied him.

18

Weber gazed at Snow. Now and then there would be a sound of some sort from the other cage that made Weber look ironic. "Poor fish. You better go in to him."

Snow looked tired out. He moved in his usual springy way; he could not help that; but his face had aged, his eyes were dull. Weber studied him devouringly. It was like Jenny. She said it tired her more because he would not get his arm up for her. There was no end to her long tiring day because of it. Neither was there an end for Snow.

19

. . . leaning back, glancing from the table to Snow, smiling a little; but when the chaplain offered to read a passage: no, no, without a comment. "Perhaps," his manner seemed to say.

His mood would turn dark.

"Fisch . . ."

"I want to stay with you, Rupert," Snow replied, tired out.

Then Jack Fisch did call: "Can't I see you, Mr. Snow?"—as a sick child in his room hears a familiar voice and, lonely, calls, not thinking the adults of the house have much to do.

"Go on."

Holy Moses. Creeping Jesus.

But these moments of exclusion were brief, and he would soon invite the exhausted young man back, darting sly glances from him to the big Bible.

The next time was important.

When Fisch called and Snow was in with Weber, the chaplain whispered conspiratorially, "I will stay with you," and gave him his deepest tired smile.

Then, as if he were falling, he dropped onto his knees and made a sign that was nervously urgent, almost peremptory, for Weber to kneel beside him: now *their* time together. Kneel by me!

"Please, brother."

"Can you stop for me again as you go out, Mr. Snow?" called Fisch.

Shh!

Snow looked up at Weber. Their blue eyes, just the same, caught, and Snow smiled, tired to death. Did he wink? Weber could see the familiar expression and knew that he was altered in the other's view, had grown as tiny as a baby, and that Snow was terrified. He pitied him.

Something else was there in the cage between them, all right; but what?

By God . . .

Weber got onto his knees beside the chaplain. On the dot!

Snow prayed:

"Eternal God, Father of us all, Thou to whom we turn every hour for help . . ."

Weber put his hand on the chaplain between his thighs, seeking the man's private arm. Snow said, "Don't!" and sprang away. He rose awkwardly to his feet and rattled the cage door until Hearn came and let him out. He went up the iron staircase without looking back.

20

"You poor young man," said Mrs. Buxton.

Yes.

She was sympathetic, yet she declared that he ought not to have done that to the girl, to Jenny.

Yes, right.

He was waiting.

"Gentlemen," he would say to the witnesses in the death chamber a few days later, "I wish you all good luck. I believe I am going to a good place, and I am ready to go. I want only to say that a great deal has been said about me that is untrue. I am bad enough. It is cruel to make me out worse."

"Oh, dear," Mrs. Buxton said.

Later he had her in the bunk with him.

And Snow came back emptied, used up. His eyes were red, as if he had been weeping. He looked in at Weber, right into the con's eyes. He said emptily, "Well, here I am."

"Yes, I see."

Snow continued to look at him. Hearn opened the cage, watched him enter, and closed it behind him. Fisch called, but the chaplain replied harshly, "Jack, I will be there in a moment. Please be patient." And to Weber: "I don't know what to say."

Weber did not speak. The chaplain looked half dead. His hands were shaking, so he thrust them into his trousers pockets. Several times he started to speak, then stopped. "Well," he said at length, "I must ask you something anyhow. Would you have prayed with me if I had remained?"

Weber nodded. He did not smile now.

Snow said, "I am very ignorant. I don't know much of anything. I have just spent more than an hour in the prison chapel, but I can't say that I am less ignorant as a result. Do you have anything to say to me?"

"No."

"Is it you, Mr. Snow?" Fisch cried.

"Shall I go to him?"

Weber shrugged, then he said, "No."

"Why not?"

"I'm number one, ain't I?"

Snow said, "Well, I'll stay with you. I think you are jealous of Fisch."

"P'r'aps I am." Why not?

"Well," Snow said, exhausted. "I'll sit beside you. Give me room."

He sat on the bunk with Weber. The con could feel the weariness and fear in the other.

Weber would do well. He would even test the straps as each one was buckled and twenty-five men watched: "Warden, just you make that a little tighter. We want everything all right, you know." Cool as a cucumber. But the first shock would not kill him. "Great God! he is alive!" "See, he breathes!" "For God's sake kill him and have it over!" Blood would come out over the man's face like sweat, and the stench would be beyond description: blood and vomit, feces, urine, singed hair and roasted flesh. He would sit in the chair for eight minutes from the time of the first shock until Nerney said he was dead, though all would claim he had been unconscious from the first second. The Reuters man would faint: men vomiting, weeping; three altogether would faint, and the rest would walk reeling down the stone corridor as if they were drunk. The Sheriff of Erie County, Weber's first keeper after his arrest and during his trial, would creep out and under the iron stairs, and lie there like a thrashed dog.

21

Now he was found! Truly. Truly and without pretense. All the bets were down, every player called, the hole cards shown, and Weber took the pot! Snow was beside him, defeated and victorious both.

It was both the same as before and a great deal better than before. LOVE and PITY—right; and Mrs. Buxton as before and as he knew her now with her scent of violets and death. There were his blazing dogs who butted their heavy affectionate heads at him; and recovered was crowned Jerusalem, city of doves; and all the cities and ways of heaven were recovered preserved for him. Trapped like a stoat in a box, he had run every way but up and been utterly unable to escape God's seductive offers. He could not help grinning at Snow. And Snow, empty but victorious, grinned too.

22

Some easing memories now, hours of gentleness. Good times came back. What would he say to being a boy again, waking on a Saturday morning in good times? That fit all right: fit like a glove.

"Everything was right for a time," he told Snow, his friend, whom he had lost and found. "Those first years in Philly after we got flooded out went nice, and I got in some regular school." He had a friend then, George Lipp, and he was the one the boy Weber would think of first on his boy's Saturday mornings in bed. What would you say to that: wake about eight, eight-thirty, nine on a Saturday morning in boyhood, keep still not to wake your brother; think of George; think of coffee and hot milk; the sun in the window; that whole neighborhood around Sixth, Seventh and Dickinson a perfect map in your mind—all the alleys and lots, stables and stores, thinking that soon you will meet your friend?

He went on about it while Snow sat listening.

There had been a fire across the street one night, and Weber watched. They carted out eight of them on shutters—six little bitty things, the two oldest of whom he had known to talk to, and two bulky ones.

What a pity!

Lipp and him once set a fire. It was nothing in that neighborhood to do a thing of that sort. And an old Jew had been killed in it.

Weber got down onto his knees, the city of his childhood and New Zion shining with equal splendor in his mind's eye. "Gentlemen, I wish you all good luck."

The Edison man, Stone, would say it was deliberate and some of the witnesses that they did not see how it could be otherwise. Stone would be wild afterwards, ranting in the basement chamber. He would declare that the signals came back mixed; that the belt on the dynamo, which he said had not been in his charge for more than half a day, slipped, so that the current was unsteady; he swore the dynamo had been tampered with, the control lights left burning on purpose to take off power, the first circuit broken much too soon and not started again promptly enough to finish Weber off. Taggart would blame Stone and others, Buxton tending to back him; Buxton would stay with his story of 1,700 volts steady, though Stone claimed it could not have been that much; nor could it have been steady.

They sat side by side on the bunk, and Weber talked. Or they prayed together earnestly on their knees. Weber constantly queried himself: was this pretense? No, it was not. It fit now. He prayed in a loud voice, unselfconsciously and fearlessly. God would hear him clear, and didn't that fit too? "Lead on, O King Eternal . . ."

Perhaps he was sly as well still, cautiously playing his game out; good! Prime! Nothing was denied, everything admitted, and didn't it all fit?

The change in Weber served to calm Fisch too.

The man came out of his cage when permitted and spoke a little to Weber. The condemned man took no exercise during these last few days; what was the point? But he took advantage of his time free of the cage, alone or with Fisch.

Fisch got his banjo out at last, fussily tuned and tightened it, then began to play on it. What a difference between the little rabbit of a man and the music he played! He would sit on a stool hunched over that thing, his narrow boy's fingers going so fast over the strings they were a blur. Just the best tunes in the world—that was all! All the ones Weber knew from his childhood and his later peddling days in the Dutch country, and a lot of others he had never heard and would have no time to learn. Prime!

All was altered—the same as before, yet better: Hearn's foot going in time to the music's beat; Jerusalem rebuilt and waiting; Fisch cheered up; the little chaplain beside him in the dusk, his beloved friend once more; whatever Weber was acceptable to God! "Gentlemen, I want only to say that a great deal has been said about me in the newspapers that is untrue, untrue. I am bad enough. It is cruel to make me out worse."

Mrs. Buxton sighed.

The burned integument of the back, on being removed, showed the spinal muscles underneath to be cooked like "overdone beef" throughout their entire thickness. The spinal cord was removed entire, but showed no gross appearances of pathological condition. Portions of its structure as well as those of brain tissue were preserved by members of the staff for purposes of hardening and microscopical examination.

He was waiting.

Dear God, he was sorry for that old Jew, though he had never thought about it before now; now he thought about it and was sorry.

He prayed, and he kept busy. There were the autograph cards to do: his name laboriously worked in pen and ink on squares of stiff paper that Mrs. Buxton had long ago supplied. For special requests from keepers and their families or from people who had sent in from the far corners of the country he would write in addition to his name the name of the prison, the date of his birth, and the date of his death. He did one of these for McDade, another for his brother in Philadelphia, and another for Buffalo Billy—William Wallace Wood was his whole name—since, though he knew for sure the man had tupped Jenny on one occasion, nothing was now denied. He wondered where George Lipp was by this time and whether there was any way of getting a card to him. Snow said he would undertake to try; he would place an advertisement in a Philadelphia paper. Thank you, thank you. Snow gave him an odd look, and he saw that the chaplain thought he might be being false; never mind, it all fit; all things false, all things true were one. What about a will? Not much was his to give, since his huckstering stuff had gone for costs and what not. These clothes were the State's. He dictated to Snow: the pictorial Bible was to go back to the chaplain's house, not to be lent again; Mrs. Buxton's book of sermons was to go back to the warden; the puzzle he worked was for old Reverend Baird; the good King suit, the watch and chain, the wallet, the cuff buttons and two gold shirt studs, the nail clip—all were to go to some discharged prisoner of Snow's choosing who had nothing decent to take away with him.

Mrs. Buxton was delighted.

Weber would wake at night, flop to the floor, and pray, while Kernahan looked on amazed.

The dogs came cringing in, their tails flailing the floor like iron chain. The Wizard gazed at Weber, that near smile on his face; you could tell he was pleased too. Weber's arm was right, and it had not been right the last time he readied for death. It was as if many parts of himself that had been always separated were now joined, and he had become, to use Keough's phrase, an entire man at last. He took Jenny at night, the dogs looking on, and prayed as he did; he took Mrs. Buxton and the old bitch, not choosing between them: couldn't either raise his arm at will? And yes, he took the sweet man too—the chaplain, his friend, took him in bed with him, hard arms together, bodies joined, lips joined.

On incising the skin over the sternum the blood which escaped was unusually dark and fluid, and remained so on exposure. There was no vermicular action of the intestine on exposure to the air or on irritation. The diaphragm extended from the fifth intercostal on the left and the fourth on the right. . . . The cranium was opened and the brain removed, the thorax opened. The heart weighed 12 ounces, the left lung 7 1/2 ounces, the right lung, which was somewhat bound down by pleural adhesions, 9 ounces.

"Dear God, I am heartily sorry for what I done to Jenny."

He had no vain and presumptuous expectation of God's favor, nor did he say within himself peace, peace, where there was no peace.

On the other hand he did not despair of God's mercy, though trouble was on every side, for he knew that God did not shut up his mercies forever in displeasure.

In the black night, eyes closed, naked he embraced his naked friend, and during the day they sat close on his bunk.

"How is your mother?" he asked tenderly, without irony.

She was entirely recovered. Snow's sister had been enabled at last to return to her own home and family.

"I'll give her a prayer anyhow, Hannibal."

No irony in the use of the name. And how was poor Belle, he wanted to know: that little girl of Snow's who was so shy and so often unhappy?

"She is as shy as ever; more so, if anything."

Just like her daddy. Weber had a special card for her and regular autograph cards for each member of the family. Snow's fear and shyness, like his daughter's, were greater than before, and Weber pitied him. The chaplain's face had become deep, eyes exhausted as if with weeping; the calm brow had a shattered look. Weber saw that his hands trembled when he came into the cage, and he felt the fear in the man.

"Dear God, ease up on Snow."

Snow's brow was embattled, eyes hidden. He looked at Weber when Weber, in prayer, had his lids lowered. He stood close to Weber or sat close to him on the bunk as the con talked of his childhood, and Weber felt the fear and trembling.

With hollow thoughtfulness Snow stared, patting a new blond mustache.

"No, I ain't crazy. It's what you're thinking, ain't it?"

Something or other.

"What?" asked the con.

"I believe *I* am half mad by now."

"And I'm entirely?"

Snow gazed with a sort of emptiness at Weber.

"It's what you think, I know. I'm telling you for the final time I ain't."

When they met and when they parted Weber shook Snow's hand; he liked that narrow hand in his; he liked its fearfulness. Sentimentally he said, "Say to Belle that a poor con asked after her special and tells her not to be so all-fired shy"—keeping his blue eyes on the chaplain's. "That goes for her daddy too." Alone he prayed for Snow and at the same time imagined he slipped his hand up between the chaplain's legs. The joke was this: he had played the cards well, and God and the cards were the same after all, as Snow had assured him; but also this: though the stoat runs every way but up, whatever he is and whatever he does he may not escape God's love. And who taught him that? That's right. Now Weber had it all going in his direction and would do his "trick" very well.

He would enter the room in the easiest manner, fixing his tie as he came, his face expressionless, the features being in repose. It would be the same while the straps were being buckled, and his gaze would range over the gathered witnesses. Buxton would have read him the warrant. "Take off your coat, Rupert," he would say and would cut off the con's shirttail with a pair of shears. "Are your suspenders all right?" "Yes, all right . . . Well, I wish everybody good luck in the world. . . ." "Well, then, Rupert, you'd best sit down." Yes, all right. "Take it cool, Rupert. I am going to stay close beside you all the while till the end." Yes, all right. The P.K. would say, "It went well, considering. It killed him right off, I say. He only give the appearance of breathing since when the bolt hit him he had his lungs full of air. He had to let it out, didn't he?" But McDade, who would have come back on the job after all at the last moment, would cry, "For God's sake kill him and have it over." And Luft, the man with the patented resuscitator, would weep because he had not been allowed to bring in his machine and use it. Dr. Nerney to the press: "The current was turned off in accordance with a previous understanding between Dr. Fox and myself (between whom and myself complete harmony existed), being asked by the warden what time should be taken, agreed to fifteen seconds and actually seventeen were allowed to elapse. When Weber's death appeared doubtful I suggested in a hurried way to the warden to have it instantly turned on again, and it was the warden who gave the order then and there." "Goodbye" was the signal to Taggart in the switch room. "Goodbye, Rupert," Buxton would say. "If Dr. Nerney had not made the mistake of ordering the current off so quickly, there would have been none of this talk," Dr. Fox would say on August 9th in New York. And another witness, unidentified: "It was all in the control room and in the dynamo, the handling of them. Yes, there might have been corrupt reasons behind it. The interests of the company who manufactures the dynamos would certainly be advanced by the defects in the machinery." "I think Weber's nerve affected those there about as much as anything," Fox would declare. "It looked to me, though, as an evidence of mental incapacity. He seemed to be without fear and helped to adjust the straps in a way that was simply astonishing." He would say, "It was the grandest success of the age, and I am today one of the happiest men in the State of New York."

23

Chalk-white, red-eyed, the warden appeared before Weber and gazed through the mesh of the cage at him. In answer to Weber's question he said, "It is to be on schedule, day after tomorrow in the early morning. Six A.M., to be exact." The warden's restless hands seemed transparent. Weber could all but see the bones in them. Everything was being revealed.

24

Buxton turned away. Kernahan and Hearn turned their backs on him as the time came. Fisch did not like to talk to him. Yet Weber asked God to go easy on them all.

25

Mrs. Buxton, the Wizard, the dogs, his first wife, Jenny, Snow— all crowded around. Snow said, "Sergeant McDade will come back, I believe. He has all but promised." Yes, for the bonus. Why not? That would be prime. Everything was to be disclosed.

26

A gentle teacher, seeing he had no overcoat in the freezing Philadelphia January, pretended she had a little boy who had outgrown his. "Here." Weber had seen it in the old clothes shop a week before.
"Take it."

27

At night naked he embraced his beloved Snow who was naked too.

28

Keough came down looking scared to death. His hand shook. "Here." These were the last kites, an epitaph among them.

Go holme dear friends wipe off your tears
Poor I must bide till Christ appers.

"Your alrite Weber. Go in peace says Jack Bell."
"Goodbye handsome. Good luck to you."
"Dear Bro.," wrote his brother . . .
". . . your aff. bro. A. H. Weber."
Everything was being revealed.

29

The man sat outside of the cage on a stool, his hat on his knees, as composed as if he had been planted and grown there. Fox, the Father of Electrical Execution. He advised Weber to bear himself like a man.

30

The new electric car system was on fire; it clanged past its stops. But the old horsecars burned too, and the animals ran on skidding hoofs, burning through the city at night. Cyclists raced past burning, mouths burning; fire and smoke came from their mouths. Men bloomed uncomplainingly into flame and went up. Cities burned around the earth, the earth giving up its dead. Ships blazed on the sea, burned down to the water; the black water rolled and hissed, the sea giving up its dead. Fire through the night in dry fields; woods blazed like torches; an egg could have fried on a city sidewalk at midnight; the ponds in parks rolled boiling, rivers steamed. Horses burned in their stables, cattle in their pastures, men in their beds; as the earth and sun kissed at last there was in every land that particular land's reserved fire. Was it Weber's turn? Right. The President's? A king's? His little child's? The poor man's? All right! Done for, yes, but only look! As men rose like sparks sucked up into the night and lifted their burnt limbs that were light as ash now (farewell!), didn't the blood and seed fall like rain across the earth to start the whole show up again for some green season in time?

31

Far from being cold, he was too hot to stay in his clothes. He stood by the cage door.

Kernahan saw him there, as he put it, "in the altogether." Not a stitch on him. Kernahan had been dozing and toward dawn awakened; something woke him, and he glanced in and saw Weber there stark naked, his penis up stiff. He said stupidly, "Here, put something on!"

Hearn was on duty too: "What is it?"

"He's taken his clothes off."

Weber was pale as wax under his clothes, with red spots all over where he had been bitten by mosquitoes and bedbugs, and running sores on his hams from two years of sitting. His muscles were slack, chest and buttocks hanging slackly. He had little body hair: a scanty bush above his penis, and a patch right in the center of the chest like a bit of cotton stuck on, a little on his forearms and calves. His hands, neck, and face were yellowish, a faint shade darker than the rest of him, his nipples dark brown. Skinny, oddly broad across the hips and narrow in chest and shoulders, with his knobby red knees and elbows, his tight grainy bag like chicken skin, the dark congested penis aloft, he stood waiting.

32

"Peter wanted to build three tabernacles there," Snow had said. "Yes, but it didn't do, did it?"

33

At four o'clock on the morning the beloved man came down the iron staircase, paused, and looked at Weber across the chamber, his face like death, while Rupert Weber sat back in the hard light of the cage. Almost everyone was there already: barber Stern, Clark, Buxton, McDade back on after all, his special guest the Erie County Sheriff, and the rest of them; the witnesses were down the corridor. Most of them there knelt with Snow and Weber. The condemned man was pouring sweat and shaking because he had begun to work hard on his death, but he glanced across another man's profile and met Snow's look; he could tip him a wink anyhow, and it tickled him to see the man wink right back. He prayed to God and then, while he was at it, threw in a prayer to the Wizard. He looked it all over, and it seemed to him to fit.

"Gentlemen, I wish you all good luck. . . ."

34

Clark stood with a handkerchief over his mouth in the State's corner of the cemetery. Safeties wearing gloves and rubber aprons opened the coffin, removed the canvas sack with Weber's dissected remains in it, and quickly tumbled the carcass into the pit of quicklime. Clark had a glimpse of it before he turned his head. It was open and empty from throat to crotch. The top of the skull had been sawed through, frontal to occiput, and removed, and Clark found himself gazing briefly into the dark cavity. There was a rubber sack of odd pieces, and that was emptied into the pit as well.

nine

Fisch

1

McDade sent word up that Fisch was misbehaving. The other condemned man had been removed from his cage to a cell next to the warden's own apartment on the afternoon before Weber's death. He had gone before the Last Sacrament was administered and been returned this noon. Just the day before the last day he had played on his banjo for Weber and that night been awakened by his acting up for the last time.

Buxton went down slowly. He felt the effects still of the draught Clark had agreed to give him: not enough to sleep, it made him feel odd, almost buoyant. He heard Fisch's screams before he was let through the heavy door at the top of the staircase that led down to the cages and paused, touching the cold wall to steady himself. He began to ease cautiously downward like an old man, the noise coming to meet him; he felt as if he were scalded by it.

McDade said, "He started again half an hour ago. I didn't call because I hoped he'd stop on his own."

The little man was standing in the center of the cage, legs apart, head hanging down so that the bald patch showed. Saliva hung from his lips. The banjo had been pulled apart and smashed to splinters, the religious pamphlets and books ripped apart, the bedclothes torn to shreds; his own clothing was torn in long rents so that blue-white flesh gleamed through it like flashes of water in the dusk of the cage. He saw Buxton and screamed immediately, doubled up, so that his head was almost on his knees.

McDade raised his voice: "I sent for Dr. Clark as well. Fisch says it smells here still, and so it does if you ask me, though we scrubbed it out well with lye soap and boiling water."

"Yes, it smells."

"Can't we move him back where he was for a few days more?"

"No, I want him here," Buxton said beneath the convict's noise. He felt odd, both tired and lightweight, as if he might float.

"He says he is afraid to be tortured as he hears Weber was. It's on his mind." He took the warden aside and handed him a folded slip of paper. "This came through."

"You can appeal on the cruel and unusual and get off, Fisch," the kite said in printed letters. "The Westinghouse Company paid to have the job on Weber botched."

"I am sorry it got into his hands. It was wrong of me and Kernahan to let it through." McDade's voice was neutral.

Fisch, hearing the day watch, raised a leg, turned on the other foot, his arms flexed and fists clenched, until he was facing away from them; the tendons in his neck stood up like stretched rope.

Clark banged hastily down the iron steps carrying his medical bag, and McDade opened the cage before he got to it, then lifted his shotgun and stood by.

Fisch stopped screaming at once; he sat on the edge of the bunk while Clark used a hypodermic right through the trouser leg into his thigh.

Warden Buxton averted his gaze to Weber's cage, which had been emptied of everything but its bare furniture and then scrubbed.

Clark said, "He wants the chaplain."

"I've sent for Snow. He can't be found just now." Buxton addressed Fisch in a loud firm voice: "We shall get Mr. Snow down to you just as soon as we can, Jack. Will you be calm until he comes?"

The little man, his head bowed nearly to his knees, nodded.

"He will be all right," said Clark.

2

Fisch sat in the wreckage of his cage. "I am sorry to see this, Jack," Snow said.

The little man was sleepy, still, hours later, affected by the drug. He leaned back against the wire wall of the cage, a leg drawn up onto the bunk, looking sleepily at the chaplain. The banjo lay twisted under the bunk; the floor was littered with paper.

Snow said, "I am sorry to see these good books torn up."

"I'm sorry too," the convict mumbled.

"It is the sort of thing Weber did."

Fisch said something too low for him to hear.

"I beg your pardon?" The chaplain was white and pinched-looking with deep smudges under his eyes, but he sat calmly, hands calm in his lap, repose in the set of his head. He looked utterly untroubled.

Fisch sighed shakily. "I said I can't tell about the sort of things Weber did. I can't help that."

"Of course not, yet this really is more like him than you. Your intellect, which is of a much higher order, is capable of understanding."

The other rolled forward and sat with his knees tight together, little hands clasped around them, head down. "I am so scared of it."

Then he said, muffled, "Won't they let me off? I can't bear it. Ain't there some way to get me off it?"

"Your appeal has not yet been heard."

The other made a hopeless gesture.

"Yes, but I tell you straight, Jack, nothing you have heard about that machine is true. It went, considering it was its first trial, very well. This talk of a conspiracy is nonsense. It is a cruel lie, and your appeal is not based on it. The machine is very good. Just look here at me a moment. Jack? I promise you it is so."

The same gesture, then a barely perceptible nod.

"Right."

Snow was sitting up straight yet looked relaxed. He had not spoken with great urgency. He turned his eyes from place to place in the cage, examining the wreckage. He picked up his everyday Bible in its leather binding, which had been resting on one knee, and held it, a finger tucked into it; he crossed his legs in an easy manner. His face was ivory white with its new mustache and the dark patches under the eyes; and his eyes, burnt-seeming, were more black now than blue; he looked older than thirty, his age, but the whole attitude of the man spoke ease, comfort, repose. He was like someone who has made an effort in a contest, done his best and done well, and then sits to get his breath in the assured rest of accomplishment, even in the expectation of praise.

"I wish they could let me off of it."

"Well, perhaps you will be."

No, no.

He kept coming back to his fear of the machine. Yet when he approached the words he needed to describe what he had heard about Weber's death, the details, he veered off; then he could not get his breath, and he would throw his head back and take rattling gulps of air like an asthmatic.

The convict stole a glance at Snow and saw that the chaplain was not looking at him. He began to move restlessly on the bunk but as if he were tied to it and could not rise. He shook his head and then could not stop shaking it. "Help me. Can no one help me?

"Oh, my dear God, oh my God," Fisch began to whisper in a hoarse voice. It was not prayer. Snow waited quietly. In a little time he would pray. He would get down on his knees and talk to God. And in a day or two more he would bring in the book, *No Darkness on the Deep,* and start on that with Fisch. They would be all right; this was a different matter from Mr. Weber; there was a mind here, and their talks would be a two-way road.

Fisch took one deep breath on another, as if there were not air enough in the world for him.

He said, "I can't tell anything. Words make me sick. What use are words if those men are going to kill me? What was the use of me being born?"

It was near midnight. Kernahan was on. There had been a racket in the prison at lights-out: the convicts objecting to the manner of Weber's death; but now it was still.

Fisch asked Snow to stay, because he knew he would not sleep.

After a while the two men knelt and prayed together. Most of the night they were silent and listened to Kernahan's steady breathing that showed he was asleep. A whippoorwill started at around two, and they glanced at each other with a kind of understanding, and listened intently to the beautiful song until it stopped at three or a little past. Snow walked home at daybreak and saw the sun rise.

It was better when he visited next. Some of his new calm and repose seemed to have gone into Fisch. Electrician Stone returned once more to work with Taggart, and when it came to it after all Jack Fisch went off in the wink of an eye without a hitch either from the spiritual or the mechanical point of view.

71 72 73 10 9 8 7 6 5 4 3 2 1